Arrival of the Snake-Woman
and other stories

Olive Senior

Longman

Longman Caribbean Limited
Trinidad and Jamaica

Longman Group UK Limited,
Longman House,
Burnt Mill, Harlow,
Essex CM20 2JE, England
and Associated Companies
throughout the world.

First published in 1989

Set in 10 on 12 Baskerville
Produced by Longman Group (FE) Ltd
Printed in Hong Kong
ISBN 0 582 031702

British Library Cataloguing in Publication Data

Senior, Olive
Arrival of the snake-woman.
I. Title
813 [F]

ISBN 0-582-03170-2

Library of Congress Cataloging-in-Publication Data

Senior, Olive.
Arrival of the snake-woman and other stories / Olive Senior.
  p.   cm. — (Longman Caribbean writers)
ISBN 0-582-03170-2
1. Jamaica—Fiction. I. Title. II. Series.
PR9265.9.S4A89   1989
813—dc19   88-37912
                                              CIP

Acknowledgements
We have unfortunately been unable to trace the copyright holders of the song
'After the Ball' and would appreciate any information which would enable us to
do so.

Contents

About the Author

Born in 1941, Olive Senior spent her early years
in Trelawny and another rural Jamaican parish,
Westmoreland. In her Trelawny village she was
one of ten children in a poor family; she was an
only child in her relatives' Westmoreland home
of comparative wealth. Moving between house-
holds, she was 'pretty much being shifted
between the two extremes of a continuum based
on race, colour and class in Jamaica.'

She began in journalism, working for the *Gleaner*
while still a student at Montego Bay High School.
She has a degree in print journalism from
Carleton University, Ottawa, Canada, and has
studied in the United Kingdom as a Thomson
Scholar. A former Editor of *Social and Economic
Studies* at the University of the West Indies, Olive
Senior is Editor of *Jamaica Journal* and Managing
Director of Institute of Jamaica Publications Ltd.

She is the author of *The Message is Change* (on the
1972 General Elections in Jamaica), *Talking of
Trees* (a collection of poems) and a reference book,
A-Z of Jamaican Heritage. She has recently
completed a book on women in the Caribbean.
Arrival of the Snake-Woman is Olive Senior's second
collection of short stories; her first award-winning
collection *Summer Lightning* gained her the
Commonwealth Writers Prize in 1987.

Arrival of the Snake-Woman

I

EVERYTHING about the snake-woman was magical from the start, even the way she arrived without our seeing, though we were all looking. I was looking especially hard for I knew more about the snake-woman than anyone except Cephas and SonSon and Moses, and I knew that Cephas and SonSon had drawn straws to see which one of them would be lucky enough to go to the Bay and bring her back to the district as his wife. And even though SonSon already had three children in the district with two different women, he was so obsessed with the idea of the snake-woman that he was willing to risk the wrath of these women, plus that of their mothers and grannies and sisters and cousins and fathers and brothers to have her. He was that taken with her. So was Cephas and so was I, though I was not old enough. But when Moses stuck out his fist with the two straws, I held my breath and wished hard that Cephas would draw the short one for then she would become my sister-in-law which was as good as being a wife or sister. SonSon winning her was almost as good though, for he was my cousin and his land was next to ours and so I would still be in close proximity to the snake-woman when she came. Waiting, I became distressed that SonSon who was lovable and kind, but lazy, was doing nothing about fixing up his house and yard for the time when he would bring the snake-woman back from the Bay.

The house had belonged to his mother who had died a few years back and SonSon since then had done nothing to stop the sagging of the floors or the leaking of the thatch or even to clear

1

the weeds from around the yard. SonSon in fact spent little time there, being usually at the home of one or the other of his baby-mothers especially Jestina who was the youngest and prettiest, or over at his ground in the cockpits which he shared with Cephas and Moses when he came up after the cane-cutting season was over in the Bay.

Moses was the first of the young men among us to work in the cane; he had been doing it for three years now, earning enough money in the season to bring home and sweeten Geraldine's temper long enough so that by the time he left she would be pregnant with another of his children. He cared for them though, and was helping Geraldine to build up a good house on her father's land and one day would settle down with her just as all the other young men settled down eventually. Only Cephas, SonSon and me knew that Moses had another family living with him during the time he spent on the sugar estate.

'Is so it does go, boys,' Moses explained, 'yu just can't help yuself. Woman down on plain like leggo beas. Yu can pick, choose, and refuse.'

But he had settled down with Trinna, a sixteen-year-old whose family lived year-round in the Bay and who was his wife for four months of the year until he came home to Geraldine. Such deviousness made me nervous but Moses had always been more daring than the rest of us. And it was Moses who told us about the snake-woman. While Trinna was young and pretty and the place was full of other women for the asking, the kind of woman he really wished he had, Moses told us, was one of the snake-women. But he couldn't have one now for he couldn't live with her in the Bay and he couldn't live with her in the district either.

'Snake-woman?' we all cried together, even I, who was supposed to be seen and not heard. In the cockpits snakes were very real to us then, hardly a day went by that we didn't see one; sometimes for sport we killed one and took it back to the district to frighten the women and children.

'That is how they does call them,' Moses said, 'from the way their body so neat and trim and they move their hip when they walk just like a snake and they don't wear no proper clothes just these thin little clothes-wrap, thinner than cobweb, yu can see every line of their body when they walk.'

Snake-women. Whai! Now we were even more confused and began shouting at once.

'Is some woman they does call coolie-woman,' Moses explained further, 'they bring them all the way cross the sea from a place call India when slavey-days end and they come with their man to work the sugar-cane when black people say no, we naa work with the cane no-more for them little scrumps a-pay. So the government bring in these people from a place call India fe work in the cane fe nutten. Them is the wutlessess set of people, though. Imagine come from so far to tek way black man work. The man them is a wicked set of beast, man. Don't trifle with them. But the woman them! Whai!'

Cephas and SonSon didn't know where India was because they hadn't been to school but I was going to school and I knew all about India and the Ganges and the Heathens who lived there, for Parson Bedlow had us pray for the Heathens of the Indies whenever we got to that part of the world in geography and in church almost every Sunday. So the snake-woman was now even more frightening to me than if she had been half-snake, half-woman which is what I had first imagined, for all of us under Parson Bedlow's sway believed that to be a Heathen was the very worst thing and now here was Moses talking about bringing to our district a Heathen-woman from the banks of the Ganges.

'These coolie-woman like nayga-man,' he was saying, 'for the coolie-man is the wussest man in the whole world. If they have a wife and she just say "kemps!" – he quick fe chop off her head. So plenty of the coolie-woman fraid of the coolie-man and want the nayga-man working in the cane to take them back to the hill with them so they can get far away from the wicked coolie-man and furtherer away from the sea which they hate like pisen for is the sea that carry them away from India.'

So Moses said. Moses told us so many stories we never knew

3

what to believe. But when he insisted that he knew one of these coolie-women who was young and slender and pretty with snake-like hips who was dying to get away from the Bay (he never told us why), both Cephas and SonSon boldly volunteered to take her. For the few weeks that Moses had remaining at home the snake-woman was the only thing they talked about when they were in their tatu in the cockpits. I noticed that they never mentioned her if others were around and I, I was too frightened to mention to anyone that we were talking about a Heathen-woman from the Ganges as if she were human like us. And I was frightened by what Parson would say when they brought her into the district wearing, Moses told us, gold bangles all the way up her arms and her ankles, gold earrings in her ears, gold chains around her neck, gold rings on her fingers and – a sure sign of heathenness, a gold ring in her nose. Any thoughts I might have had that she was not a true Heathen vanished when I heard this, for Parson Bedlow had been very explicit about one thing and it was the Heathen's sinful lust for gold – 'Their tinkling ornaments about their feet . . . The chains, and the bracelets . . . the ornaments of their legs . . . the rings, the nose jewels . . .' – exactly as it was in the Bible!

And yet, I didn't care. I was already half in love with the snake-woman, with her nose ring and tinkling ornaments and her outrageous, barbaric ways; I could hardly wait for Cephas and SonSon to go with Moses to the Bay and bring her back to the hills.

Although I never heard the men tell anyone of their plans, people must have suspected that something was about to happen, for there was an expectancy in the air and after the men finally left – and there was nothing unusual about his friends accompanying Moses back to the Bay – everyone seemed to be excitedly wondering when Cephas and SonSon would return. Part of their interest was because the two men were making purchases for everyone in the district, but in my own excitement and my guilt, I saw them waiting expectantly not for their pots and their cloth, their salt, machetes and files, but for a snake-woman to arrive.

Every night in the yard next to SonSon's I could hardly fall asleep, night after night waiting for the squeak of the hampers on the donkeys that would signal that SonSon and Cephas and the snake-woman had arrived. At that sound, I planned to rush out for my first glimpse of her. But the nights wore on and they never came and I would fall asleep until dawn and my mother waking me. My first thoughts were always of the next yard but it was too dark to see anything and I had to be up and about to tie out the goat, fetch wood and water, then I had to come back to the house and sit at the table and have breakfast as my mother insisted, another irritating thing she had learnt from going to classes in housewifery which Parson's wife Miss Rita had organised.

The day was well advanced before I was able to shake my mother off and head for the bank of sweet-smelling khus-khus which separated our yard from the next — to be greeted by the disappointing spectacle of an empty house. But one morning my heart somersaulted for there, framed in the doorway, was the snake-woman herself. Who else could it be? She was wearing her gold bangles and necklaces and earrings and a nose ring and a garment which seemed like bits and pieces of spiders' webs draped all about her from head to foot. Her head was covered so I didn't immediately see her hair which Moses said was black as a sink-hole and straight as Miss Rita's own, though the snake-woman's skin was as dark as ours. And so it was. After the initial thrill though, I felt a little let down, the snake-woman was so small, her body as slender as a child's, and since she stood so still in the doorway I had no idea what her hips were like and if she moved like a snake when she walked or even like a daughter of Zion. I wondered if Parson had had a premonition of the snake-woman's arrival for that Sunday he had preached fulsomely, warning the men against a specific temptation:

'The daughters of Zion are haughty, and walk with stretched forth necks and wanton eyes, walking and mincing as they go, and making a tinkling with their feet.'

But what really held me even far away were her eyes, which were black like a dark night and took up half her face and when

5

I finally came close and looked into those eyes, they seemed so faraway and sorrowful that I felt I was looking deep into the Ganges.

But before that moment came she vanished from the doorway. In a little while, I could tell from the smoke coming from the lean-to that she had got a fire going. How wonderful, I thought, the ashes have been cold in the fireplace for so long yet here's a snake-woman kindling a fire. Who could have imagined this happening in our district? But she soon reappeared from the kitchen with two large calabashes and began to look around the yard frantically. How like SonSon, I thought, not to have filled the barrel with water and to sleep late on such a morning. And though I was fearful and shy of the snake-woman, of what Parson, everyone in the district was going to say, and though my heart was pounding just as it did when Parson was about to take me up in my lessons, I couldn't stand the way that that frail figure stood lost in the early morning and without conscious thought I found myself moving from my hiding place behind the khus-khus and walking confidently towards her.

II

And so I became Miss Coolie's guide and friend. Everyone came to call her Miss Coolie for that is what SonSon and Cephas called her and in all the years I knew her, I never knew her name except for Gertrude which Parson gave her when she was baptised and which was never used by anyone except him and his wife. Later, when all the children including her own got older, they came to call her Auntie Coolie and finally in her old age, surrounded by her children and grandchildren in the Top House with a fat and very contented SonSon beside her, dressed once more in her gold bangles, rings, earrings and nose ring, we all respectfully addressed her as Mother Coolie. I don't think that anyone ever knew her Indian name or anything about her, partly because she hardly spoke at all. It was as if, crossing over the mountains to start a new life, or perhaps even earlier when she crossed the seas, she had left behind all that reminded her of the old, shed her identity and her history, became trans-formed into whatever we would make of her, our Miss Coolie. I never knew whether she spoke so little because she was naturally very reticent or whether she never really felt comfort-able speaking English, or whether in her early years of hardship, isolation and exile she had got into the habit of not speaking.

In any case, it was a long time before anyone spoke to her, except for Cephas, SonSon and me. For the entire district shunned her. Partly because of Parson and partly because of SonSon's baby-mothers. It was one thing to go from woman to woman in the district, it was quite another to bring one over the mountains, and a Heathen-woman at that.

Everyone was nevertheless quite curious about her, and my mother, our house, became popular with visitors at all hours since they might, by stretching their necks, get a glimpse of the strange woman. She herself was never seen on the track or down at the crossroads; the only time she left home was for wood or water and she developed an instinct for doing these things when nobody was about, as if she had no desire to flaunt her presence.

The most frequent visitor to our house was Jestina, SonSon's youngest baby-mother, who sat on our kitchen step day in day out with Noel the baby playing in the yard around her, while she helped my mother with some household chore and 'throw-word' and 'cut-eye' at the 'coolie-gal' next door. At these times I was ashamed of my mother for encouraging the women's gossip, making herself popular and important by passing along little tidbits that would then be retailed the length and breadth of the district and, to my everlasting shame, even passing on things about Miss Coolie that I had innocently mentioned to her.

'Mi dear, she don't eat like we yu know she make a little bread thing she call roti and some yellow thing she throw on the food now call curry. Is Ishmael tell me so for he in and out of her kitchen all day long. I tell him Ishmael don't eat from that woman yu don't know what Heathen thing she feeding you. Next thing it slow down yu growth and cork up

7

yu brain and the smell on yu clothes when yu come out of that
woman kitchen! Is a Heathen smell that alright. God know what
she doing to SonSon . . . but the boy deaf from him two eye
pitch pon that woman.'

'Nuh so Heathen witchcraft stay.'

My mother never actually forbade me to go over to Miss
Coolie because I realised long afterwards I was her pipeline –
and so the district's – into Miss Coolie's house. But I was too
young to know that at the time. I just listened to the women's
gossip, terrified that one day my mother would prevent me from
going next door. But she never did.

The way Miss Coolie dressed was a constant source of amaze-
ment.

'She don't have no real clothes like decent Christian people
'tall 'tall. All she does have is them square of cloth like sheet
which she doan iron, she just wash out and heng on the line.
Ishmael say she does call them saree.'

'Thin and sinful little piece of cloth.'

'But some of them pretty-caan-done you know.'

'Vanity of vanity all is vanity.'

'Selah.'

'An her hair long down it long down it long down clear pass
her bottom. Never know hair could long so.'

Everyone was convinced that Miss Coolie was a witch like
Ribber Muma that had caught SonSon while he was sleeping
and ensnared him with her long hair and that one day SonSon
would come to his senses long enough to get Papa Dias to give
him something to relieve him of his crosses. But first he would
have to get away from the woman for she was *tying* him by the
yellow thing she was putting into his food.

But SonSon did not look like a man possessed or unhappy.
And he laughed at their hints in his loud booming laugh. At the
best of times SonSon was a happy man, his very happiness
making him insensitive to the needs of others, impervious to the
currents swirling around him. So the happiness Miss Coolie
brought him banished from his mind any thought of her own
happiness or unhappiness. And she made him so happy. Here

he had a woman who was devoting all her time to seeing to his needs, who kept his belly full and his house clean, who presumably made him happy at nights and who asked for nothing, who was silent and smiling all the while, and who was so hard-working.

For as if to confirm the charge that she was a witch, in a few months Miss Coolie had transformed the yard from a weed-filled place to a magical garden in which she grew all kinds of things which at the time were new to us: garden eggs, Indian kale, strange peas and beans, tulsi and herbs which sent fluffy flowerheads into the air from which she harvested seeds which she kept for teas, for seasonings and for treating ailments. Did she bring all the plants with her from the Bay, from India, and how did she get them to grow in a place where nobody else had grown anything except coffee and cocoa beans, yam, dasheen and eddoe, red peas and cassava, cho-chos, skellion and thyme, mint, ginger and sage? Her kitchen was so full of wonderful smells and colours, mixes and powders which she parched and pounded and stored away in tiny baskets she wove herself.

With all the work she had to do, what with looking for wood, carrying water, looking after the house, washing, cooking and working in her garden, Miss Coolie had begun to change. First she took to wearing her hair in one long plait down her back. Then little by little she discarded her jewellery, first the rings and anklets of gold, then the necklaces and bangles till she was down to one or two bangles, her earrings and her nose jewel. But whether she was digging in the yard or carrying water or firewood on her head, she continued to wear her graceful saris, light as Anansi web.

I was with Miss Coolie as often as possible and more and more I found myself talking to her though she never made any reply except to smile at me or nod encouragingly to let me know that she listened. To her I confided my dreams, my hopes, as she nodded her head or frowned in sympathy. How Parson Bedlow said I was so bright and fuelled my desire to do well in school, to go away and study, to become someone other than a labourer on the land or a cane-cutter like Moses. What I

9

would study, what I wanted to become I did not know, but I wanted more than anything else to cross the mountains and enter the world outside.

I never knew if Miss Coolie really understood anything more than the tone of my voice, the urgency, but she showed great interest in my books, tracing her fingers over the print, looking at the pictures, and she was enchanted when I took an atlas I had borrowed from Parson, and showed her first the world where our tiny island and India were located so far apart and then a map of India itself, like our island coloured red. Her eyes immediately filled with tears and she turned away from the mortar and wiped her eyes on the edge of her sari and went hurriedly on with her pounding.

But even as Miss Coolie was the one to whom I confided my dreams, my hopes, she also now became the greatest threat to my future.

III

Miss Coolie became the chief demon in Parson Bedlow's pantheon, replacing rum drinking, fornication, smoking, cursing, lying, wife-beating, idleness, backsliding, taking the Lord's name in vain and some other sins we had never heard of before. Now he had a real Daughter of Zion, Whore of Babylon to rail against, there was new fire in his preaching: Woe Woe Woe he intoned all day Sunday and nightly when we had prayer meetings. His pleas for bringing the Heathen into the fold became even more impassioned as he prayed for God to touch her soul.

After Miss Coolie had been a few months in our midst he went and called on her, but she hid trembling and he had to content himself with praying loudly against her closed door. His wife tried next, but Miss Coolie ran and hid again until Miss Rita, accompanied by several ladies of the church, turned sadly aside. Of course there was no appealing to SonSon for he himself was beyond redemption. My mother and other church members tried over the years, people who by that time Miss Coolie had become used to, but while she didn't hide from them, she listened without a word and when they were finished, she would hand around her sweets and mint tea and they would eat and drink and at the end of it, leave without knowing what they had achieved.

Her hard-heartedness enraged Parson Bedlow. For a while he saw me as the instrument for bringing her to Christ for who better than an innocent child, he said, to touch the Heathen's heart. But my problem was that I had more interesting things to discuss with Miss Coolie than her soul, and in any event I had begun to wonder if she were a real Heathen after all, she was so good and kind to me, so hard-working, so totally serene and uncomplaining in the face of her loneliness and adversity. When I did not succeed in converting her, Parson Bedlow lectured me about spending so much time with her and then he threatened me. Only the boy of the purest heart, he said, the finest character, the strongest will, would be sent outside to school, friends of idolators would not be considered. I knew that I was the only boy being considered, the one on whom Parson Bedlow and Miss Rita were concentrating all their energies. For they kept saying that they wanted me to become a native missionary, one that would go outside to be trained and carry on their work, take the word of God back to Mount Rose or to Darkest Africa even, if it were God's will. Still, I worried that he would carry out his threat of not sending me away to school. So I hit upon the strategy of telling him that I was praying earnestly for Miss Coolie every day, counselling her, waiting for God to guide her. But I knew this to be a lie for I was doing no such thing, and this made me feel baser than before. I became even more anxious now that Parson should catch me out in lying, spent sleepless nights wrestling with my conscience now that like Moses I was practising deceit. But I would not give up Miss Coolie for she needed a friend and I had been chosen. And her coming by some mysterious and still ill-defined process was helping me to see that there were other paths, that there were alternatives beyond the pure and narrow path to

11

Heaven of Parson Bedlow or the road to Hell that everyone said was Moses's.

But I was profoundly disturbed now that because of Parson I was caught in such a web of deceit, of lying, though when I got older and was able to see things more clearly, I realised that Parson Bedlow from the start had turned all of us, the whole district into deceivers and liars, though this was far from his intention.

IV

Long after slavery ended and the old-time white people died off or moved away, Parson Bedlow became the first white person to come back into the district. And why had he come? Who was he really and how did he get there? His origins, his coming, were as mysterious as Miss Coolie's. The old people like Papa Dias, Grandy Maud and Mother Miracle who were around from slavery days said that Parson Bedlow was very different from the old-time white people who owned Mount Rose, the whole district which was in coffee at one time, and who had brought the black people here as their slaves. These old-time white people were more like the black people than Parson Bedlow because they were out in the sun all day and burnt brown and drank rum and coffee and smoked jackass rope and cussed bad words worse than the black people. And they worked hard too, even the white women. They worked side by side at Top House yard with the black women making starch and chocolate and soap, parching coffee and drying bisi, salting down the meat the men brought from hunting in the cockpits into the big barrels of brine, sewing all the clothes that everyone wore. These old-time white people didn't eat much better than the slaves and didn't act much better either, but they didn't treat them badly.

Papa Dias would tell me, 'Before slavey-day end, bwoy, Mount Rose nayga walk up and down the place like they free, free already. And when they do anything now, the backra people fraid to say anything or punish them for only four a-dem lef and they drink rum and coffee and smoke rope tobacco nuh fool, the woman and all and from days gone by the white man a-sleep, a-sleep with the nayga-woman so the nayga-woman could facety all they want with the white man for whole set of white-black people, mulata people walking about Mount Rose as living proof of what the white man been up to. And with all the mulata people around who could call the backra people Puppa and Grannie and Cousin and Sister if they wanted was to, everything at Mount Rose mix-up, mix-up now and the young white people couldn't stand how Mount Rose lonely and far from everything and I don't think they was making money for all that, and you know how white people love money, so the young white people tek-time gone, tek-time gone and we never see them again. And the rest of them die off. So lo-and-behold when slavey-day end now is only the two white woman lef, Miss Ersie and Miss Min and they very old and they live at Top House till they die off and only the nayga people and the mix-up mulata people lef to take care of them in their last years and bury them. And is so all the old-time backra people done gone.'

No one even knew how the old-time white people had found their way to that spot in the first place, Mount Rose was so far into the bush, right on the edge of the cockpits with one trail leading south into the Bay and the other to Newcastle, a little market town to the north. And the old-time people, Papa Dias, Grandy Maud and Mother Miracle, said that when-all-is-said-and-done the black people at Mount Rose were better off than black people anywhere else, not like these nayga people down at the Bay and other places where they grow cane.

Papa Dias say, 'Oh is a shame, a shame, bwoy. Those nayga people that work in cane real slave, worse than slave, they treat them like animal. Long after slavey-day done everywhere else, they still like slave down there working in the cane.'

Mount Rose people looked down on all the people who worked in the cane and were very displeased when Moses announced that there was no living for a young man in the district for people were hardly making any money from coffee

13

at that time, and left for the Bay to work in the canefields. Nobody expected to see Moses again for they thought he was walking into slavery and they were very surprised when he came back looking fat and well with money in his pockets. But people in the district still didn't trust anything the other side of the mountains, especially the Bay, and their fear of what happened on the sugar estates was not the only reason. The real reason why the old people were frightened was that one day they expected white people connected with the old-time white people from slavery days to come riding in from the Bay and claim the land of the old Mount Rose coffee plantation which the people had been living on and working for two generations now since slavery ended and had taken for their own.

So when this white man and white woman appeared suddenly one day everyone was frightened because they believed that they had come at last to claim the land. But from the start nobody was sure, for the first thing which this strange white man who was dressed in black from head to foot did was to get off his mule with a big black book in his hand. By this time the news of their arrival had spread, for Easton who lived by the cross-roads had blown the shell the minute he sighted them and everyone in the district who could move came running. And the white man took off his hat and his hair and his face were smooth like baby-corn and white like dry starch as if he had no blood. Some of the littler children started to cry and he looked around at everyone one by one until all fell silent, and then he said to the nearest person who was Papa Dias who had been creeping nearer and nearer all along to get a good look to see if he looked like the old-time white people, he said, 'My son, what is the name of this place?'

Papa Dias said, 'Mount Rose, Massa' though he was trembling like all the other old people and didn't really want to tell the man. And then, instead of doing what everyone expected, which was to say, 'I have come for the land,' this strange white man said,

'My Children, Let Us Pray.'

And he kneeled straight down in the dirt in his good black clothes.

People already knew about this praying business from Mother Miracle so they began to relax a bit and bowed their heads, but the strange white man stayed on his knees and talked for about an hour straight, calling down the grace of God on his ministry to Mount Rose and he prayed so well that nobody got tired and everyone was impressed that a man could use words so. And that is what made them think that he was not connected with the old-time white people. But still, they couldn't be sure, for as Papa Dias said, 'You can't trust any white man for even if a white man don't set out to tek weh what you have, as you turn round so, whatsoever is rightfully yours just swips gone out of yu hand into se him own – you don't rightly know how and braps! ol'nayga turn slave again.'

Much to everyone's surprise, this strange pair, Parson Bedlow and his wife whom we called Miss Rita, showed no sign of leaving and gave every sign of settling in Mount Rose, sent, they said, to bring light to our darkness. And they rented the old Top House from the Ramsay family who little by little had claimed it as their own because they were the ones who had looked after the old-time white people to the end.

Now Papa Dias was the most respected man in Mount Rose for he was the oldest man and he had the most land and he know more than all the rest for Ol'Massa had taught him everything, how to figure and how to write things down in a book. In slavery days he was the man who took the coffee to the Bay packed into crocus bags on a string of mules for the trail was too narrow and rocky then for carts and he brought back the mules and jacks laden with anything that was needed – barrels of herring and bolts of cloth and rum and tools and hardware for Ol'Massa. So from his early youth he was a travelled man and he knew the ways of the world. But he was respected and feared for an even more important reason which was that he was a man of *knowledge* and he could do *workings* and could divine fate from throwing bisi the way his old Oyo grandfather had taught him, some even said he could summon Shango God of

15

Thunder and do many such things. And his mother's mother was a mulata, the daughter of one of the old masters, and she had passed down to him the white people's eyes and his 'puss-eye' in his black skin enabled him to see far and at nights too, people said, even behind him. And they said it was because of his eyes why Ol'Massa trusted him.

Until Parson Bedlow arrived, Papa Dias and Mother Miracle were the real rulers, in charge of everything that happened in Mount Rose. She had also travelled in the old days though she wasn't Mother Miracle then. She and Grandy Maud and Miss Mirts who died before I was born were the first of the higglers, carrying things to Newcastle to sell that she cultivated on land which her father had set aside for her, for he was one of the old masters and he had given her her freedom long before the others. So Mother Miracle used to lord it over everybody and act real proud and haughty for she had her own land, she wasn't squatting like the rest of them and she was free to come and go as she pleased from even during the days of slavery. But the Sixty Revival came sweeping over the land, came as far as Newcastle though Mount Rose people never knew about it they were so backward. And in Newcastle one market night as Mother Miracle stood in a crowd around a revival band, a woman who was in the spirit reached out and hit Mother Miracle, and so the spirit entered her body and she began to dance too and it swept her into the band and by next morning it had swept her away from all who knew her.

Long after everyone had given her up for dead she came home one day, clapping her hands, singing and praying and falling into the spirit even as she got to our crossroads. She never answered to her old name but said that they were now to call her Mother Miracle for when God was ready he planned to work a great miracle through her and he had told her to have the name ready. And everyone laughed at her and called her Mother-Miracle-Name-A-Ready. Whenever the spirit took her, she would walk up and down for weeks at a time, preaching and testifying, warning and predicting, even as far away as the Bay, and she never bothered to cultivate her land after that and totally rejected her old ways. And people said 'How are the mighty fallen,' and made fun of her and said she had got mad down in the Bay and thought they even knew who had caused the madness. So nobody heeded her warnings, not even when she predicted a terrible drought.

And when the drought did hit, in truth it was worse than anything anyone had ever experienced: the rivers, every spring dried up and people had to go into the cockpits and cut down water wiss to get something to drink, they even raided wild pine for water. And then one day Mother Miracle said she would fast till God showed her a sign that he would send water again. And she started to fast and people were getting so desperate for the crops and the animals; even the children were beginning to die, that they started one-one to go by her house and sit outside while she fasted, to sing softly the songs they had heard her singing and to pray with her, and then more and more people kept coming for in truth most people by that time had nothing to eat anyway and nothing to do. And somebody started to cut a notch in the cedar tree for each day of Mother Miracle's fast. And when it reached nine Mother Miracle suddenly rose up from the bed on which she was lying and shouted, 'I have seen the light. Thank you, High Massa'. And right away in the middle of the night, she walked straight to a spot in her yard and holding a hoe, she spun around three times and jammed the hoe into the ground and started to turn the soil. People thought she had gone mad again but she told them that God had told her to dig at just that spot and she would find a spring of clear water that would never go dry so long as someone believed. And people by this time were so hungry and demoralised that nobody even bothered to laugh at her as she kept digging. It took her a long time for the earth was very hard and nobody understood where she got the strength after fasting for nine days and nine nights and she wasn't a young woman either. But day by day Mother Miracle was digging a deeper and deeper hole and the crowd at her house now got bigger day and night for some people never bothered to go home at all. By this time Mother Miracle had dug a hole so deep she had to use a ladder to climb in and out and it was getting harder and harder for her to even lift the hoe – everybody could see that – much less throw the dirt out of the hole. So she agreed that the men could help her with clearing the hole but she had to do all the digging herself so the men started to let down a bucket to get the dirt out of the hole. And still Mother Miracle kept digging. 'I never got my name for nothing,' she would say, 'High Massa working miracles through me. The land will be green again, the sick will be healed, water will flow again, unbelievers believe.'

By this time everybody wanted desperately to believe, as if Mother Miracle's miracle was all they had to cling to. But Mother Miracle was weakening, everyone could see that, and one day those who were leaning over looking down into the hole suddenly saw her keel over and fall and she lay there for a long long time and never got up again. They had the devil's own time getting her out of the hole but they managed it for by this time she weighed so little and she was cold and stiff as if she was already dead, and they laid her out on her bed and tied sinkle-bible on her head, rubbed her down with coconut oil and spirit weed. And people sat by her bedside singing all night as if it were a wake though she wasn't dead yet, but nobody believed she would survive the night. And though everyone meant to keep awake, little by little the singing died down and they all fell asleep, the people inside and the people outside the house. As dawn came one person outside awoke and heard a sound like water bubbling up bubbling up so he touched the person next to him and said, 'Tell me what you hear,' and that person listened and said, 'It sound like water bubbling up' and he touched the next person and asked him the same thing and everybody listened and said they heard the sound of water bubbling up. But they all thought they were going mad with dreams of water like Mother Miracle, hearing what they so desperately wanted to hear, so nobody looked into the hole.

When daylight came, everyone was astonished to see Mother Miracle walk out of her house looking as fresh as ever, dressed in a clean white robe with a blue sash, wearing a clean blue head wrap, carrying her staff and walking strongly like a young girl and Mother Miracle started to sing, 'Shall we gather at the river,' and everyone found himself singing too, getting up and falling behind Mother Miracle all in procession, even though nobody really thought about what they were doing. Mother Miracle led them in a march counterclockwise around her yard seven times and the singing got stronger and stronger for everyone forgot about their hunger and thirst, the burnt crops and dying children, all were singing as lustily as they could as they marched behind Mother Miracle. And after they had circled the yard seven times she led them to the hole she had been digging and nobody felt any surprise at all to find that the hole was filled with crystal-clear water that was still bubbling bubbling for hadn't they all heard it during the night?

Believe it or not that is how Mother Miracle found water. In the middle of the worst drought in history. Hit a spring of the purest, cleanest water. And that is how everyone at Mount Rose survived the drought. And afterwards the people all helped Mother Miracle to build a temple by the spring and when water was flowing in the other springs again, this became not a spring of ordinary water but a holy place and people came from far and near to be healed in Mother Miracle's spring. And she stopped walking up and down and getting into the spirit at the crossroads as if she was mad and settled down as a balm lady, conducting services at her yard, *reading* people for what ailed them, treating them with herbs and bushes and holy water.

In a way Mother Miracle and Papa Dias were competitors for they both dealt in spiritual matters though of different sorts. But there seemed to be a need among the people for both kinds of services and both of them had a great deal of work and there was no animosity between them, indeed, since they were among the few old people still left from slavery-days, they were the best of friends though they never discussed their work with one another.

So when Parson Bedlow arrived, in a similar line of business, as people saw it, everyone watched expectantly to see what Papa Dias and Mother Miracle would do before deciding how to act themselves. But they surprised everyone by not doing or saying anything against these new white people. In fact they supported them in everything they did from their first efforts to start a church – Papa Dias becoming one of the deacons – invaluable to Parson and Miss Rita in every way. Mother Miracle never missed a church service, on Sundays or weekdays, adjusting the time of her own services to fit in with Parson Bedlow's. It was as if they had decided that the best course in dealing with the strangers was to get as close to them as possible, and they were still unsure about their position regarding the land. Papa Dias and Mother Miracle had the most to lose for even though Mother Miracle's father had given her a plot of land, he had never given her a *paper* to go with it and everybody knew that the white people and the law which supported everything they did only dealt in *paper*. And then some people said that Papa Dias and Mother Miracle supported Parson's church only because they wanted to learn as much as possible about his operations.

There is no doubt that with Parson's coming both Papa Dias and Mother Miracle fell on lean times for after Parson had established himself, his preaching about devils and idolators and false prophets and miracle workers started to penetrate people's consciousness. Of course we never knew if Parson knew who Papa Dias and Mother Miracle really were, for even people who were in the bosom of the white people were careful what they told them. But a lot of people stopped patronising them and clung to Parson and his wife because aside from religion, they also brought with them things like medicine and books and opened a school for the children and got all the men to put up a church building and then a meeting hall which was brightly lit at nights with special lanterns they got from America which gave a light which seemed as bright as day. And all in all they became the centre of a new life, a progressive, modern life in Mount Rose. They were connected with churches in America which was like magic for these people sent them barrel upon barrel of goods for the district. It took thirty mules and donkeys and almost all the men to move their things from the Bay over the mountains.

And some people who had been the main supporters of Mother Miracle's church started to back-bite her and testify against her though they never called her by name. They were more afraid of Papa Dias and never openly attacked him though they began to shun him with hints and whispers. Part of the reason why Papa Dias seemed to be losing power was that from the time Parson Bedlow came everyone thought that Papa would have tried to get rid of him by *working* something, but whether he tried and failed or never tried at all for reasons of his own, we never knew, for Parson and Miss Rita showed no signs of leaving. Day by day, year by year, they dug themselves deeper and deeper into the life of the district, began to exert a kind of control over everyone and everything that was different from the way Papa Dias and Mother Miracle had managed us. For while Papa Dias and Mother Miracle in fact knew everybody's business, they also recognised the private character of their ministries which were partly aimed at meeting individual human needs and were by nature, private and confidential.

Parson Bedlow, on the other hand, conducted his ministry publicly and openly involved everyone. He knew who was committing adultery with whom and would call up the guilty parties, if church members, for public confession, chastisement and punishment. He knew which of the young girls was pregnant before anybody else and who the baby was for, and if the father was free, would force them to marry. In fact the first thing Parson did when he got going was force all the church members living together 'in sin' to get married. My own father and mother ended up with one of his marriage certificates. At first people were frightened by the possibility of public revelations of their actions and strived their utmost not to offend, the earnest ones forsaking the 'evil-doing', the more hypocritical simply becoming more careful. But all dreaded the worst punishment which was being read out of church for those outside the church could not benefit in any way from Parson's largesse and were regarded as poor souls, lacking in ambition or totally beyond redemption – these latter were usually the younger men like Moses, Cephas and SonSon.

In short, getting and retaining church membership became the badge of those who regarded themselves as the most progresssive and who, most importantly, were also the chosen ones who would make it into Heaven, escaping the everlasting punishment of Hell fire which began to be even more real and frightening than anything Papa Dias could invoke. So for the first time since the days of slavery and the coming of the people to Mount Rose, there was division in the district. Not that all had been entirely peace and love before. Of course there were quarrels and family feuds, violence and evil, but nothing that could not be put right again, nothing that had ever divided the whole district, that pitted friend against friend, household against household, brother against sister, parents against children.

Of course Papa Dias and Mother Miracle who were older and wiser than all of us probably understood that sooner or later some people would get tired of certain aspects of Parson Bedlow's church. For aside from interfering in the everyday joys of living and making everyone twice as secretive and anxious about everything they did, Parson's church did not allow its members to dance and sing and play the tambourine and drum and clap and shout and get into the spirit the way they did at Mother Miracle's. And they probably had known that everyone would find out sooner or later that while Parson Bedlow's medicine was useful against things like whooping cough, ring worm and running belly, yaws and vomiting sickness, sprain foot and sores, it was of no use at all for certain things. It could not take away the effects of grudgefulness or cut-eye, counteract spitefulness, cure love-fever or the malignancies of guilt which showed itself in mysterious ways, could not provide relief for a man who had lost his nature or who was *tied* because a woman had sprinkled something on his food. For these things, depending on the type of illness, its suspected origin and the cure required, one had to seek out Mother Miracle or Papa Dias or increasingly now as Papa Dias got old, his nephew Esau whom they said Papa had taken as his apprentice and was teaching how to divine fate the way his Oyo grandfather had taught him. Only they could prevent or get rid of certain things, or counteract them.

So little by little the church members began drifting back to Mother Miracle, walking the steep path up Durance Hill to Papa Dias. Neither of them commented publicly on these things but soon most of the church members were back to their old way of life or rather, they now had two parallel ways of life, one highly secret, just as they had had in different ways, when the old-time white people were around. Everybody continued to attend service and fawn over Parson and his wife, saying yes-bucky-massa, no-bucky-missis to everything they said and it wasn't only because they were white. It wasn't because of their church building with glass windows – the first we had seen, their pretty coloured pictures of Jesus and his disciples and people in the Holy Land which they handed out to the children, the free Bibles for everyone though most people couldn't read, the free cloth from America which Miss Rita and the women sewed into clothes for the children, their gifts of whistles and fee-fees at Christmas time, their medicines and store-bought things in their house, their threat of Heaven or Hell, which really gave them their authority. No. What bound the people to them was the book-learning which they were passing on to the children in the little schoolhouse which they built. Nobody in the district wanted to give up this thing, the magic that was contained in black and white squiggles on paper, the sweetest sound from the schoolhouse of little voices repeating over and over in chorus, 'Twice twos four. Twice fours eight. Twice eight sixteen'. This was the true source of power, this learning to add, multiply and divide, to do sums in one's head, things which in the old days only some of the old-time white people and Papa Dias knew how to do and they hadn't offered to teach anyone.

With all of this learning that was going on and the excitement it was causing, both Mother Miracle and Papa Dias were finding more and more that they had a new clientele, parents bringing their little children either for a guzu from Papa or a bush bath and reading from Mother, and sometimes both, to ensure that they would learn their ABCs and pass from Book One to Book Two, from Book Three to Book Four; that they could carry the entire multiplication tables in their heads and draw the right squiggles on their slates or write in their exercise books with pen and ink without blotting, that they could learn the difference between rods, roods and acres without twisting them up and, most important of all, that they should do well in their examinations or at the very least, that they should behave and do nothing to provoke Parson Bedlow to throw them out of school, which he sometimes did.

My mother was one of those who believed passionately in this schooling the way she never believed in anything else, and though she was one of Parson's strongest supporters and no longer attended Mother Miracle's services, she became so anxious over me that she did have consultations from time to time with Papa Dias and made me wear again as I did as a small child a red string with a guzu round my neck, this time to protect me against those who were jealous of my success. And she took me to several readings and baths to strengthen my brains, at Mother Miracle's. All – as Parson did – divined for me a wonderful future, but my mother knew that this wonderful future hinged on not upsetting Parson and Miss Rita. So my mother was especially anxious that among those who refused to follow Parson from the very start was her own big son Cephas, her nephew SonSon and Moses who was also a blood relative. And she felt it keenly all her life and believed that it reflected badly on her that she could never pray with enough conviction to change their ways. And when SonSon brought the snake-woman into the district, into the very house that his mother, her elder sister, had died and left him, Mother's grief knew no bounds and she more than anyone else prayed earnestly with Parson for the salvation of the temptress brought into their midst by those who had travelled to the Bay and so knew the stink of the corruption of Babylon.

V

Of course at the time these things were happening I never had these thoughts about Parson and what was occurring in the district; like all church members I too, passionately, literally, believed in the visions of Heaven and Hell which Parson so vividly portrayed for us, accepted without question everything he said. Night and morning I prayed and wrestled with my conscience for I earnestly wished to go to Heaven. More than anything else I wanted to go away to school and become an educated man, a missionary or schoolteacher, to *elevate* myself, as Parson used to tell me.

Fortunately the struggle with my conscience over my association with Miss Coolie eased somewhat when Miss Coolie had her first child, for attitudes towards her began to soften then. Though SonSon had planned to be around when the time came and had even alerted Nana who delivered all babies, it was just like SonSon that he was not there and Miss Coolie was alone when their first child was born. I hadn't seen her that morning and went by her house and was just about to call out when I heard a cry like a goat kid which startled me because it sounded as if it were coming from inside the house and still no sign of Miss Coolie. I called and called from the door and got no answer but there was this crying again from Miss Coolie's room. I stepped inside the hall and looked in and in the half darkness I made out Miss Coolie lying on the floor. Before I could say anything she said, 'Ish, call Mama', and I responded only to the urgency of her voice and I fled for my mother and then for Nana and SonSon.

My mother and all the women immediately rallied around Miss Coolie. For a baby, after all, made all women the same. And when the news spread, people, men and women, came from all over the district, leaving on the doorstep gifts of dukuno, bammies, plantain and sugarhead though Nana allowed no one to see Miss Coolie and the child for nine days, nor fresh air nor sun to touch them; during that time they had to lie in the darkness of the room together, for that was the only way to protect the frail new soul from evil spirits passing, from catching 'baby cold' which is what took careless mothers and babies away.

Under Nana's care, no such thing happened for she made certain to cut the navel string with special scissors used only for that purpose and carefully hidden away until the navel was cured, to wash the newly-born in water in which rum and a silver threepence provided by the father had been thrown, to dress the navel with nutmeg, dose mother and baby with a heaping teaspoon of castor oil each, to see that a new broom was brought and hidden away in the room to be used later to sweep out all the dust which accumulated under the bed for the nine days so that it could be specially disposed of. During these nine days Nana was in total charge of the household, doing all that needed to be done for the mother and child, at the end of which she would go away happy with another job well done, a silver dollar and a bankra of food. Only Mother Miracle was allowed into the room when she came bearing a calabash of her precious holy water. And on the ninth day Miss Coolie emerged from the room with Biya, for that is what she called her son from the start.

Biya was loved by everyone, he was such a lively, handsome little boy with his father's sense of mischief and fun. By the time he could walk, Biya was all over the district, in and out of people's houses, even in the homes of Jestina and Dina, SonSon's other baby-mothers. Nobody saw anything wrong in that for the children were all brothers and sisters after all and Jestina had been among the first to visit after Biya's birth, shyly bringing a gift of bisi and nutmegs for her yard was one of the few places at that time with those trees, and her own little son Noel to visit. Whether or not Miss Coolie knew at the time who she was, she greeted her as graciously as she greeted everyone else, pressing on them her little cakes flavoured with aniseed, her mint tea and tamarind balls.

When Biya was two years old, Miss Coolie and SonSon cut his hair for the first time and 'turn thanks' to the district by giving their first curry goat feast. I was the envy of all the children my age for I was in at this historic event from the start, appointed myself Miss Coolie's chief taster, helped her parch and pound the spices and herbs, helped her grate the coconuts, as excited as everyone else who was going to taste curry goat for the first time for although we all ate goat meat, this was the first time people of the district would get a taste of Miss Coolie's strange yellow food, though, if truth be told, both SonSon and I had been boasting for years now about how good it was. Miss Coolie was going to kill not one but two goats, a small fortune, and SonSon was digging his best yams. His friends brought food too, and piled up in their yard were great bunches of bananas and plantain, mounds of coconuts, and yampies. The women came early with their largest bella-guts and jestas and cala-bashes, caught up fires in the yard, peeled huge piles of bananas, made dukonu and fu-fu, threw the plantains and yampies into the hot ashes to roast. SonSon's friends from the evening before had started to build a dancing booth of plaited coconut fronds which the girls decorated with flowers as if for a wedding. I spent part of the morning with my friends gathering banana leaves, which we left in a wooden trough of water to keep fresh, so that later we could cut them into neat strips to use as plates at our curry goat feast.

And so Biya pulled Miss Coolie more and more into the life of the district. For one thing he was given to straying – just like SonSon, everybody said – and Miss Coolie was always having to go off in search of him, calling his name from house to house. But though she was mixing with people more (many now addressed her by her name and she by theirs) this did not mean that Miss Coolie had come to be totally accepted. Parson still held her up to church members as the epitome of sin and the devil incarnate for now she had brought into the world a little Heathen soul that she refused to redeem, refused to bring into the church to be baptised. And what, Parson asked, would happen if this little soul should die without baptism? It too would fall into the pit of Hell, would suffer the fires of damnation. What kind of woman who called herself a mother would risk bringing such suffering on an innocent little child?

I shuddered at the thought and wondered myself at this paradox. For there was no doubt in my mind that Miss Coolie loved Biya with a love that was so intense it was almost frightening to see. It was as if Biya had been sent to compensate for all the unhappinesss, all the suffering of her life. And I wondered how she could run the risk of his falling into the pit of everlasting fire, suffering forever by her negligence in not bringing him to Christ. But still, I could never find tongue to broach any of this to Miss Coolie.

And then something happened that brought all of these contradictions to a head for me. Biya got ill, some sickness that all the children came down with and at first Miss Coolie tried with all the herbs and powders that she had successfully used before to cure his ailments. When he got sicker, Mother Miracle came, blessed him with holy water and advised jack-inna-bush and fever grass for tea, a bath with mashed jointer three times a day and a rub down of wild sage and warm coconut oil. But that too failed and Biya got worse. The October rains had just ended and as usual brought chill nights and early morning mists to the cockpits, and left in their wake a district full of people with colds and fevers, coughs and chills, wheezing chests and other complaints.

But soon everyone realised that this was not the normal sickness that children got from the rains for some of them started to die and not Mother Miracle, not Papa Dias could save them. But several little children had not died, were in fact recovering after their mothers had taken them to Top House where Miss Rita gave them a medicine mixed in a bottle, a thick pink liquid, and she had created a room for the worst children so that they could stay there and with the help of some of the women nursed them day and night. And these children were getting better and more mothers were bringing their children in to get some of the white people's medicine. So when I looked at Biya and saw him wasted down to nothing but his huge eyes, I screwed up my courage and told Miss Coolie about Miss Rita's medicine and urged her to take Biya there. Of course I had not considered the implications of any of this but Miss Coolie obviously had for she adamantly refused to even consider it. But Biya was not getting any better and even my own mother suggested that she should take him to Miss Rita. Miss Coolie by then had nothing to lose I suppose so she finally wrapped up Biya and I set out with her for Top House, Miss Coolie almost running now in her haste. When we got to Top House there were other mothers with their children sitting on a bench outside Miss Rita's sick room and nobody seemed surprised to see Miss Coolie there. They eased down on the bench to let her sit but nobody said anything, all the mothers silently bound together in their anxiety over their children. And Parson Bedlow was there too; he and Miss Rita were inside examining the children one by one, giving them medicines, deciding which were the ones too sick to go home. And people kept moving up on the bench as the person nearest the door went inside and soon Miss Coolie was at the end of the bench nearest the door and when the mother inside came out I went to Miss Coolie and touched her hand and she was trembling so much I almost had to push her into the room so they could look at Biya and Miss Rita saw her first and her eyes widened in surprise and then she smiled and held out her arms to take Biya and lay him on the table beside her on which they had spread a blanket. And then Parson Bedlow who had been sitting by the table writing notes in a book looked up and saw Miss Coolie and it was as if he was seeing a duppy, as if the devil itself had entered his little hospital.

'No!' he shouted, jumping up and screaming, 'Get that woman out of here! We cannot have her here! Unclean!'

'But dear – ' Miss Rita said in the soft voice she had, 'her baby . . .'

'No, no, no!' Parson continued shouting and he looked so angry I thought he would burst. Miss Coolie stood there a moment as if frozen, caught in the posture of handing Biya over to Miss Rita, and then she recovered herself, pulled Biya tightly to her body and dashed through the door, rushed off at such a pace that I had a hard time keeping up with her, down the path which was still slippery from the rains, through the coffee piece, round by the grasspiece, through more coffee and up the hill again to our land and hers. Miss Coolie moved so fast I had no time to think of anything and when I caught up with her she had already dashed inside her house and put Biya down on the bed, was pulling down bundles from the rafters, putting on, I noticed, several of the bangles she had taken off before. 'Catch donkey for me, Ish,' she ordered in a manner she had never used before in speaking to me. But without question I went out and caught and saddled the donkey, the same one SonSon had brought her in from the Bay on, and she came out with a bundle, with bedding and clothing and started to put these inside the hampers and I was not sure what she was doing and thought she was leaving us forever. Then she dashed back inside and came out with Biya all bundled up with only his tiny face showing and I helped her lay him on top of some clothes in one hamper and tie him in and she put a few things together in the other and mounted the donkey. 'Don't worry, Ish. A come back. Biya come back. Gone doctor.'

Doctor! That meant the Bay for that was the only place to find a doctor. Miss Coolie couldn't be serious about going to the Bay alone. A day and night journey for a man and so lonely no one ever went alone, certainly not a woman. 'I'll come with you, Miss Coolie,' I cried, and without waiting for an answer I ran to our house to tell my mother but she wasn't there and by the time I got back to Miss Coolie's she had gone down the hill, alone to the Bay with Biya. And I would never see them again!

The thought was unbearable and I started to run after them but they were nowhere to be seen and I sat down under the mango tree by the path as great sobs tore through me and I cried and cried for Biya who would die and burn in Hell fire everlasting. I cried for Miss Coolie who would not be able to live without Biya and would go to Hell also and I cried for me for I didn't know where I was going. Until somewhere in my crying I remembered SonSon who was never around when he was needed for he had gone to his ground that morning to dig food and should be coming back any time now, of SonSon who loved Biya as much as Miss Coolie and Miss Coolie more than anyone, SonSon who was good and kind and who was my, everybody's, friend. So instead of running after Miss Coolie I ran over to SonSon's ground, stumbled over rocks and tree roots, picked myself up over and over and kept runnning and crying at the same time until I got to the ground and found SonSon and Cephas in their tatu there, about to dig into a big pot of red peas soup which they always cooked when they were over at their ground. And I blurted out my story.

After that I didn't remember anything much for days uncounted, for I fell into a kind of stupor, only heard afterwards how SonSon and Cephas packed their donkeys and packed the big pot of soup into one of the hampers on SonSon's donkey, so he and Miss Coolie and Biya would have something to eat on the way for he set out immediately after Miss Coolie. And how Cephas carried me home on the other donkey for I was half dying myself and put me to bed where I stayed for days on end for I was delirious and feverish and knew nothing except fragments in which Miss Coolie and Biya were burning in Hell fire everlasting and Parson Bedlow kept pushing them back each time they tried to climb out, crying, 'No, no, no'. Even after I came back to my senses I would lie there listlessly day after day, unable to pull my limbs, my thoughts together, unable to face anything, least of all school and Parson Bedlow.

And then one day there was a vaguely familiar voice calling me and I peeked and there was SonSon smiling at me.

'Ish! Ish! Talk to me Ish bwoy.'

He was shaking me so I opened my eyes.

'Ish bwoy, what kind of foolishness this, man? Miss Coolie send plenty how-di-do and send sweetie clear from the Bay for you. But if you don't get up bwoy, A gwine eat it me own self. For A have a hard time keeping it from the ants bwoy.'

So Miss Coolie was alright. And Biya. I must have asked aloud.

'Oh Biya fine. He send love too. All day long Biya asking after you, "Ish, Ish." All day long he looking round calling for Ish.'

Then SonSon told me how Biya was in the hospital in the Bay and how he almost died and would have died if they had not got him there in time. And the doctors were keeping him in the hospital for a while longer till he was completely well again and Miss Coolie was staying there till he got better.

The hospital! The place we had a dread of so! Nobody would ever dream of going to the hospital it was so far one would die reaching there; in any event the hospital was regarded as a place of pure death. So till Miss Rita had come, everyone had relied on Mother Miracle or Papa Dias to cure all ailments and Nana to deliver and care for babies and if all failed and the patient died, it had been so willed and no one could prevent it.

And here Miss Coolie had come and broken another taboo, had taken Biya to the hospital and he hadn't died and was going to be well again. For I was sure that SonSon would not look so pleased and smiling if that were not true. And for the first time in weeks I felt like stirring myself, started to take an interest in the world around me, got out of bed, took a few steps, ate a few mouthfuls of food.

In later years of course I realised that my sickness was entirely of the soul, a way of coping with the things my mind refused to dwell on. And as I started to get better, to re-enter the world, so I was forced to face the painful truth of what ailed me, of how to reconcile Parson's preaching about charity and love and the ministry of Jesus and his disciples who reached out to all, of the Ten Commandments and loving one another, with his behaviour to Miss Coolie and Biya. And I vowed that I would never be like Parson, never follow in his footsteps and be a missionary. I never wanted again to have anything to do with his life, his world, his book learning. I would stay here and be like the other men: I would plant ground with Cephas and SonSon and Moses, hunt birds and coneys and hogs in the woods, dance the shay-shay and chase women. I no longer wanted to elevate myself or for Parson to elevate me. For I came to the belief that my hurt, my pain, had come about because I had overreached myself, I had set myself above the people around me, had in so many unkind ways begun to act as if I was better than they were, even my own parents. I was puffed up with pride in my new knowledge, my book learning, the special attentions from the white people.

So even though I was getting better and stronger, though my mother fussed over me, tried everything to make me well including the ministrations of Parson and Miss Rita, Mother Miracle and Papa Dias at different times, I continued to lie most of the time in bed. For I had decided not to go back to school and I hadn't yet worked out a way to tell her without breaking her heart. So I continued to malinger, playing the invalid, and I probably would have fallen permanently into that life if Miss Coolie and Biya hadn't come back, Biya looking pounds heavier than when he left us, as merry and tricky as before. Miss Coolie seemed thinner, older and had dark circles under her eyes. But her smile was as tender as ever when she greeted me.

'Tenky, Ish,' were her first words and I wondered what she was thanking me for, I who was as bad as Parson Bedlow. 'Now I get you better.' And I found myself pouring out to her all my pent-up feelings, feelings that I could share with no one else, about Parson, about getting above my station in life, about never going back to school but joining Cephas and SonSon at their ground, about how to break it to my mother.

Miss Coolie seemed unperturbed at my recital as if she had heard it all before. She listened without comment and then she said in the same voice she had used in ordering me to catch the donkey,

'Ish, you go back school.'

'No,' I said.

'Yes,' she said as if I hadn't spoken, as if she were speaking a dream aloud. 'You go back school. You go far as that man send you. America.' (For Parson's latest plan was to send me there.) 'Ish, you know what? You turn doctor.'

What! I was startled. A doctor? In those days none of us had even seen a doctor. We knew who they were, of course, the white men who took black people's bodies and cut them up into little bits, sawed off this and that as a 'cure' and did God-knows-what with the pieces. People to stay away from. Of course I knew about the Beloved Physician Luke but he had no connection in my mind with these doctors in the Bay.

'They cut up black people body and do all kind of terrible things to them,' I blurted out. 'And is white man business that. You ever hear black man is doctor?'

'Ish, I trying tell you. Have a black man, well, more a brown man, at hospital. Ish, he save Biya life. Nice man, very nice man to me and Biya. He, all the white doctor too, helping cure people. Not kill them. Fix them up good good good. Look Biya.'

I had to confess that Biya looked very well.

'And Ish, I tell this doctor, this brown man bout you. Bout my little friend going America to study. He say to tell you Ish, turn doctor too. Say plenty black man turning doctor now. World changing.'

For a moment I was tantalised by the thought of being able in some mysterious way to wave my wand over sick children like Biya and cure them, of being able to make the lame walk and the blind see, for such were my only ideas of medicine. But then I remembered that all this would not be possible without the collaboration of Parson Bedlow. He was still my passport to anywhere beyond the mountains. And I had not, could not bring myself to forgive Parson Bedlow for saying no to Miss Coolie, to Biya that day. But when I told Miss Coolie this she said simply, 'Ish, I forgive him. You forgive him too. You need him help you. Only one that can help you. You must turn doctor so you can help people like Biya and me. People like your Mama. Poor people.'

I said nothing for a while.

'You know what your problem is,' Miss Coolie continued, 'You don't know nothing bout world, you not even been to Bay. Why, little Biya know more than you now! When you get out there you find world full of good people, bad people, all kind of people. And you have to learn deal with alla them. Same as you get all sort of thing out book. Good and bad thing.'

And with that she went out and left me. I was astonished that Miss Coolie had spoken at such length as well as by what she had said and I turned it all over very carefully in my mind. Thought about what she said about my becoming a doctor. About my being able to come back and help people. And that I couldn't do it without Parson. I had to resolve in my own mind what I wanted to do. What I wanted to be. And so between Miss Coolie and Parson they again forced me into dissembling. For I went back to Top House and to school, told myself that I could pretend with Parson for as long as he could help me, never to let him know my true feelings, my questionings, my uncertainties, my fears.

When I was up and about moving around the district again, I realised that the incident with Miss Coolie had hurt Parson badly. People were still talking about it. Several, including Mother Miracle, left the church as a result. Mother Miracle said, 'Jesus said "Suffer little children to come onto me". And he turn away a sick child. No. That is not a man of God.' And she began to hold meetings again at her balmyard at the old times, not caring whether or not these clashed with Parson Bedlow's services for she was finished with Parson Bedlow. And several people chose to go with Mother Miracle and be baptised by her all over again. And so her church started to grow again though by this time everyone said Mother Miracle was at least a hundred years old.

And Parson said nothing to me when I returned to school but I noticed dark circles under his eyes the same as Miss Coolie's as if he had been suffering too and his manner had softened somewhat, and I began to perceive him for the first time as a human being like all of us, began to wonder if he too had feelings, if he suffered, if he had conflicts like me, of what life must be like for a man of such ability, such learning, to spend his life among people who were illiterate, ignorant of the world outside. And I wondered what drove him, what made him dedicate his life to such as we. And whether he felt badly afterwards over his treatment of Miss Coolie. Of course he never referred to the incident but he devoted more time to me than ever, spent long hours teaching me now higher mathematics, Latin, Greek, for he was still fixed on my being a parson. I said nothing but absorbed all he had to teach me like a sponge. Now the learning was an end in itself, separated totally from my soul, from the possibilities of Heaven and Hell. I got so absorbed with learning that I saw Miss Coolie and Biya less and less; for the first time since Miss Coolie came, she ceased to be the centre of my consciousness. Now I had a new infatuation.

One day when I was coming home from lessons she called me over and I realised guiltily that I hadn't spoken to Miss Coolie in a long long time. But her greeting was as warm as ever.

'Hi, Ish, How lesson going?'

'Fine, Miss Coolie.'

She invited me to sit and have mint tea and aniseed cakes, took up my books and looked at them, ran her fingers over the letters as she always did, turned them over and over, examining them, and I could tell that she had something on her mind.

'Ish.'

'Yes Miss Coolie.'

'Biya going turn lawyer.'

'A lawyer?'

As usual, Miss Coolie expressed herself with certainty. She was announcing it in the same way she had announced that I would be a doctor.

'Yes. Then he will get *paper* for the land. For everybody. Then white man can't come and tek it weh.'

I didn't know that Miss Coolie knew about these concerns.

'Ish.'

'Yes Miss Coolie.'

'Biya five year old now.'

'Yes Miss Coolie.'

I wondered where this was leading.

'Know what that mean?'

I shook my head.

'Time for him to go to school.'

Of course. Parson took the children in for the infant school, a play school really, from the age of five. I didn't say anything for all the old anxieties had come flooding back over me.

'Ish, you think the man there will let Biya into school?'

And although I knew she knew the answer to that, I knew she wanted to hear it from me. So I told her no.

She was silent for a long long time.

'Miss Coolie,' I said timidly; for the first time since I had known Miss Coolie I was feeling shy with her, so I got the words out in a rush. 'Miss Coolie all you have to do is accept Jesus Christ as your personal saviour then you can get baptise and join the church. Parson would let Biya into school then.'

'I know,' she said quietly.

I knew then that this was my big moment, the occasion for me to say the right words and bring Miss Coolie into the fold. But the image of Parson and Miss Coolie together was still too disturbing to me, a violent image even, an image that had shaken my own faith, my own beliefs to the core and now I did not even know what I myself believed. So I did not say anything. Indeed, I got so anxious, broke into such a sweat, that I could no longer bear Miss Coolie's presence and churlishly fled, my books getting heavier and heavier as I ran over to our yard, feeling old beyond my years, confused, carrying burdens that I still felt unable to cope with. Almost, Parson would have said, a lost sheep. And I kept away from Miss Coolie as the time got nearer and nearer for Biya to go to school.

VI

Sunday again and we are sitting in church and Parson is about to raise the first hymn indeed he has announced it: 'The King of Love my Shepherd is.' We are waiting on him to lead off with the first line so we can repeat it and he actually starts:

'The King of Love my Shepherd is, his goodness faileth never,' and he raises his eyes from the book and looks to the

back of the church and his voice peters out and he is staring
as if seeing a duppy and although he immediately catches hold
of himself and starts again: 'The King of Love my Shepherd is,
his goodness faileth never,' there is no answering voice from
any of us for we have all turned to follow his gaze and our
mouths drop open, every one, for there in the doorway is Miss
Coolie holding Biya by the hand. But the shock is not only at
seeing Miss Coolie in church but at seeing Miss Coolie wearing
for the first time what everyone calls 'decent people clothes'. She
is dressed for Sunday now like the other women all in white –
long starched petticoats and skirt, a long-sleeved, high-neck
blouse and white headwrap that totally hides her hair. She has
removed all her jewellery – her bangles, her rings, earrings and
nose ring. And she is standing there uncertain, all of us uncertain, suspended together, waiting for a word from Parson
Bedlow, a full minute's hush while I hold my breath until I am
about to burst.

'Praise God from whom all blessings flow,' intones Parson
Bedlow, smiling at Miss Coolie, completely forgetting that that
is what we sing at the close of service.

'Praise God from whom all blessings flow,' we sing, turning
back to face him like puppets.

'Praise him all creatures here below.'
There is a shuffling at the back as people move down on a bench
to make room for Miss Coolie and Biya.

'Praise him above ye Heavenly host
Praise Father, Son and Holy Ghost.'
Our voices soar higher and higher in praise, thanksgiving,
jubilation. And so Miss Coolie and Biya are welcomed into our
church.

And when school opens, Miss Coolie is among the proud
mothers leading her child by the hand to be registered; Biya like
all the other little children, crying lustily all the way.

VII

Long afterwards I realised that Miss Coolie must have taken the decision to join the church while she was down in the Bay, must have spent the time there giving thought to her new life, the way ahead and how best she could deal with the situation that faced her. She must have had the new clothes made up then for she could not sew, brought them back with her, waiting to screw up her courage to enter Parson's church.

Her baptism was a turning point in Miss Coolie's life for it marked the stage when she began to firmly control her own destiny. It wasn't only because she was now fully accepted by Parson and the church members. It was as if she herself had decided to accept totally the life into which she had been thrust, to become fully a part of the district, to cast off the mantle of outsider and outcast. So for a long time she never put on her saris and jewellery again. And early one Thursday morning as the women were leaving on the long trek to market at Newcastle, as they came to the point where Miss Coolie's track joined the main path, there she was with her loaded donkey, and as she fell in with them in the darkness, she looked no different from the black and mulatto women of the district carrying their goods to market.

During this time Miss Coolie began to have her other children, one almost every year until she had seven girls. It was as if she had been waiting to see how Biya would fare in this strange land before commencing childbearing again. But Biya remained her only boy. And from the start she said that the first girl Najeela would be my wife, and she said it with the same sweet certainty that she had said all the other things, so that too would end up coming true. And she arranged marriages in this same casual but definite way, having no problem finding husbands from among the best young men in the area, in Newcastle and even in the Bay for all her lovely coolie-rials.

As her family grew she built a new house, a wooden one next to the old two-room thatched hut which she had first lived in, and this wooden house grew year by year. One of the rooms became a shop for as she travelled to market, Miss Coolie somehow found the means to acquire a little surplus of all the things we needed and had to buy – oil and flour and rice and salt, later exposed our taste to butter instead of coconut oil, to sweet-smelling soaps, powders and pomades, toothpaste instead of chewstick, healing oil and liniment for our pains, bolts of bright cloth, thread, ribbons, boots and shoes, hair-straightening combs and skin bleaches, the first sewing machine.

At first it was not a real shop, Miss Coolie just kept a few things at her house to sell if a customer came by. But people got used to the convenience of having things to hand right there in Mount Rose and the operation became a proper shop, run by SonSon in her absence, then by Biya even when he was very young, later by all the girls in turn, in time encompassing sons-in-law and grandchildren. The shop – our first – blossomed until – and this was well into the future – Miss Coolie constructed a large building at the crossroads to hold her various operations. Drygoods, grocery, bar, butchershop on Fridays, grain store and produce dealing for she was the one who negotiated the sale of our citrus and coffee, nutmeg and pimento, ginger and arrowroot with the middlemen who came from town to buy these things for resale abroad. Miss Coolie was into so many things – her garden, her goats, her higglering which soon turned wholly into shopkeeping that people began to murmur at her success. For although she gave everyone credit she charged that little extra, and people found that although they could always go to her for a loan, they ended up paying back more than they borrowed. And this was foreign to them. So although Miss Coolie was providing the district with services which they never had before, people who were used only to reciprocation in exchanges now found that this no longer held true. Miss Coolie was 'in business'. That became her favourite phrase whenever anyone said or hinted anything, 'Ai mi dear. Is business.' As if 'business' had a separate existence outside of human agency.

As for Biya, Miss Coolie scrimped and saved in the early years and got him into high school in the town and supported him over the many years until he became a fully qualified lawyer. And though Biya practised in the Bay, people said he was tied to his mother's apron strings for he never married and came home every minute and walked around the district in the same old way, stopping to drink and chat and laugh at everyone's house, admiring their daughters and, if truth be told, 'falling' a lot of them. But everyone continued to love Biya not only for his ways, but also because the minute he became a lawyer the first thing he did was get titles for all the people who had originally settled on Mount Rose. Biya kept his promise and made sure that all the old people could go to their graves knowing that no one could come and take away the land. And Miss Coolie and Biya bought the piece with Top House from old man Ramsay, paid him a fair price, no matter what people say, and he was happy to sell for he could then indulge himself to his heart's content in the rum bar till now he was back at Top House living in a lean-to and being a virtual yard-man for Miss Coolie. And it made me ashamed all my life that Biya had done more for the district than I ever did, despite my promise to myself, to my parents, Miss Coolie, Parson, everyone, that I would come back to be the first doctor in the district.

I had left with their hopes, their prayers, if truth be told their little gifts of money they could hardly spare; it was as if everyone was investing his dreams, his hopes for his own children, in me. And I did go to school in America and from there to England and I didn't come back for a long long time for after I qualified I told myself that I needed to gain experience and when finally I came home and went back to Mount Rose, I trembled with shock and shame at the smallness, the meanness of it, the backwardness, the hopelessness. And I stayed long enough only for Miss Coolie to marry me off to Najeela for that arrangement I hadn't the heart to change and had no other plans, before I fled back to the city and a job with the government medical service.

I have had no regrets about Najeela because she is very beautiful, the image of her mother, and has made me a suitable wife, for although Miss Coolie had not bothered to educate any of her girls beyond elementary school, she brought them up properly and taught them how to do everything that would be pleasing to a man. Although as I got older and began to rise in the ranks, I sometimes wished that I had a wife who was more educated and outgoing, like the wives of the other professionals who would at least converse with each other. Mark you, Najeela has never shamed me like some of those women for she never opens her mouth in public. Miss Coolie has instilled in her such a sense of duty that even though we have got to the stage where we can afford several maids and she doesn't have to lift a finger, she insists that she should still see to everything. She prepares my favourite dishes herself and personally looks after our children and she is the thriftiest soul on earth, she refuses to spend money on anything we don't need; indeed, manages all our financial affairs for she is far shrewder about these matters than I am.

And it is because of these very children that I could not keep my promise to the old people and go back to Mount Rose for how could I set up a practice in such a backward place? I want to be sure that my children grow up in the city, that they have the right start, that they will not have to go through the pains of adjustment that I had to go through when I finally left Mount Rose. I want my children to acquire from birth the knowledge, the confidence that people now need to cope in this new century that has just begun. For the world is changing so fast. Even Mount Rose. So many people have died: Mother Miracle, Nana, Papa Dias, many of the younger generation too including my own mother, Parson, Miss Rita are long dead too, now a brown man runs their church. But he could never hold sway over the district as Parson once did. For one thing, there are now several churches to choose from, the government has built a school, roads have been cut connecting us to other towns and villages and people are travelling in and out of the district all the time; many have been travelling to foreign lands, Panama and Costa Rica, even America, to seek their fortunes.

Every time I go back I marvel that the most prosperous

citizen of the district by far is the former outcast, Miss Coolie. Now she is living at Top House where the old-time white people, then Parson Bedlow, used to live, a house built to last of solid mahogany and cedar shingles but which over the years had fallen into decay, become a 'ratta-castle' even. Miss Coolie has restored it, added to it, built gardens and water tanks. She needs a big house for her family has grown larger with the passing years, various daughters, sons-in-law and their children live with her, working in the business. Then there are SonSon's 'outside' grandchildren through Jestina and Dina, and more and more of Biya's children with the local girls – all who want to come find a place in Miss Coolie's household.

And I wonder how the people of the district view Miss Coolie now, but of course what anyone thinks no longer matters for she has wealth which nowadays will triumph over everything. Yet she herself is still the same soft spoken, smiling, quiet lady she has always been. She has reverted to wearing saris again, ones with gold and silver borders now, put back on her bangles, her rings, earrings and her nose ring; put a red spot on her forehead to show she is a married lady (for Parson Bedlow had forced her and SonSon to be properly churched once she converted). And she gave all her daughters Indian names and adorned them with gold ornaments as soon as they were born and forsook the church as soon as the government school came in.

I discovered that this gold was the secret of Miss Coolie's wealth, her capital, for when I was going away to school she made me a gift of a heavy gold bangle and told me, 'Ish, never sell this. Keep it and anytime you need money go and pawn it. But never never sell.' She had to explain to me what a pawn shop was but many times I had occasion to take the little gold bangle to one and it made me understand better how Miss Coolie managed, how she had started out living in a two-room thatched hut the same as the other women and managed to so surpass them. But it was more than that. For she also had from the start an understanding of the world that the rest of us lacked, a pragmatic drive that allowed her to dispassionately weigh alternatives, make her decisions and act, while we still floundered around in a confused tangle of emotions, family ties, custom and superstition.

Her arrival represented a loosening of the bonds that had previously bound her, that bind all of us to our homes. Cut free from her past, she was thus free of the duties and obligations that tie us so tightly to one another, sometimes in a stranglehold. She became a free agent with a flexibility that enabled her to soar above our world which was still structured around our faith in the bisi nuts of the Oyo grandfather, Mother Miracle's holy water and Jesus' second coming. A flexibility that enabled her to 'do business' with family, friend, or the white men that came to buy produce from her. Miss Coolie, in short, is our embodiment of the spirit of the new age, an age in which sentiment has been replaced by pragmatism and superstition by materialism.

Going back home on occasions I like to watch Miss Coolie the businesswoman, the matriarch, smiling and at ease, surrounded by her large family. And SonSon that pleasant, easy going man to whom she still caters hand and foot but who repays it with his undying devotion. And I wonder what would have happened if Cephas had been the one to pull the short straw from Moses' hand that day over by the tatu, for Cephas has turned out to be a manager himself, a tyrant of his household. How would he and Miss Coolie have fared together?

And I speculate how each of us is shaped by circumstances we do not control, how my own life was shaped by Parson Bedlow, by Miss Coolie's coming; otherwise I would probably have ended up no more than one of the village rum-heads. And yet, perhaps few of us are really born out of our time. Perhaps Papa Dias and Mother Miracle were born into one world and could have functioned in no other. Even Parson Bedlow himself, for who of the present generation would listen to him now? And sometimes I am still unsure of my own self, of who I am, of where I belong, still feeling halfway between the old world where my navel-string is buried, and the new, unable to shake off the old strictures, the sentimental attachments of my earlier upbringing, not feeling, like Miss Coolie, at ease enough to shift fully into the relentless present. And this is why I sometimes sit and write down the things that happened in the old days, so that my children will be able to see clearly where we are coming from, should they ever need signposts.

Miss Coolie now. I will always wonder about her. For I find her still as great a mystery as when she came as our snake-woman, so little of herself has she revealed. Has she found happiness here in the heartland of a small island so far from home? Does she accept without regret the new life she has built since she decided for reasons known only to herself to accept SonSon's offer to bring her over the mountains? I can never be sure, for there is the evidence of the saris, the red dot, the Indian names. And sometimes, when I look into her eyes, I can still see the Ganges.

The Tenantry of Birds

WHEN she went on to the verandah after coming home she noticed immediately that the bird tree had no tenants. How strange. The bird tree used to be fully lived in all year round. The rather bedraggled tree at the bottom of the garden near the gully she had always thought of as a bird tree or tenantry. It seemed to have no year-round dwellers but a succession of temporary visitors who came regularly at the same time each year, claimed a branch for a while, then left again for another season. So busy was this tenantry that it reminded her of the game they played as children:

Room for rent
Apply within
When I run out
You run in.

But while lesser birds might come and go unnoticed, the star boarders were the pecharies, a pair that came each year and built their nest in the highest branches from which they could hurl themselves screaming, from time to time, on to the head of some luckless straying bird or even other tenants on the lower branches who dared to get too close. Particularly ferocious was their assault on the kling-klings, who flew along in untidy and noisy flocks from tree to tree before settling in amused disorder in one or even several of the adjacent trees. They reminded her of rude children at parties who refused to sit at table or be organised for games, who ate too much and were ungainly in habit and bearing and yet who always seemed to her so fortunate and carefree. The pecharies particularly disliked the kling-klings and reserved their most spiteful curses for them.

The kling-klings – rough, uncouth, chattering and uncaring merely shrugged them off and headed noisily for another tree. But the pecharies would continue to attack until the kling-klings were driven out of the garden.

She was fascinated by the tree, by the birds in the garden and the pecharies in particular, for their fierce protection of their young, their togetherness and most marvellous of all, for the way they gave their young ones lessons in flying and shrieking before pushing them out of the nest, tenderly hovering to catch them if they fell. But they never did.

Sometimes she became so engrossed in watching the antics of the birds that Philip would come out of the bedroom dressed and ready for class and find her there with a silly grin on her face and laugh at her foolishness, her sentimentality about the birds.

When they had bought the house, Philip had wanted to cut down the tree which he found unsightly, but she protested. For she had seen the nesting pecharies from the verandah from the very first day and the tree held a peculiar fascination for her. It was as if it were something from a more primitive, less contrived location than their garden, that had wandered into the wrong place and flourished there.

With the house came a beautifully kept garden and Philip ensured that it continued to be so. Not that he himself did any gardening but he was good at giving orders to Vinton the gardener about the straightness of the hedges, the greenness of the lawns, the trimming of trees and shrubs, and before going to work usually made a morning inspection of everything. Philip's idea of a garden was a showplace of straight lines, of symmetry, of everything exactly in its place. She hated the garden for these reasons and because it had precisely those plants which she most disliked, the same ones that had been in her mother's garden and the gardens of all the people she knew – hybrid crotons, poinsettia, gladioli, dahlias and gerberas, red roses, pink anthuriums, allamanda and ixoria. She would have preferred a wilder, more informal kind of garden with huge spreading trees and a riot of flowers in bloom all year round looking as if they grew naturally there, like her aunt's garden in the country. But in those days she had been afraid to argue with Philip, to venture an opinion, to suggest anything, and the garden which was smug and trim like the gardens of their affluent neighbours, stayed as it was.

Only the bird tree remained to mar its perfection (on sufferance, for Philip still threatened its death) but it was out of the way at the bottom of the garden, seen only from the upstairs verandah outside the bedrooms. It was a shabby tree; really it was two trees. There was a timber tree which she could not identify and growing against it to the point where it almost enveloped it was a leguminous bush of rampant growth. Perhaps the competition stimulated both for the strange tree combination got taller and taller, wilder and more unkempt as the branches tangled together: a perfect tenantry for the birds.

Early mornings she would get up and while Mirelle got the children ready for school and before she joined them for break-fast, she would sit out there by herself and watch the antics of the birds around. So she knew the minute the john chewitts arrived each year; when the loggerheads darted to grab the bird peppers; when the mockingbirds sang. Sometimes after Philip and the children left she would go back to the verandah, straining her eyes and ears to see and hear the birds. She knew that she was wasting time when she should be up-and-doing, but she never did much of anything anyway. She found that her life now fell into a pattern of lethargy about everything, and watching the birds was the most satisfying, the most seductive part of her day that, put her in touch with something pure and free, unnatural and unfettered, something that demanded nothing more than the delight of her senses.

Not that she knew much about birds. In fact all she knew was what she had learnt during the long-ago summers she had spent with her aunt and uncle in the country. There she would be overwhelmed by a houseful of disorderly cousins, some resident, some visiting like her, who could be as noisy and brash as the kling-klings, as swift and quarrelsome as the pecharies. But they all startled her with their knowledge: how to set traps for birds using flour and straw and how to play dolly pot and moonshine darling, how to set spells on lizards to get them to stand still for minutes at a time and to call out 'Green Bush. Green Bush. Green Bush' to make wasps go away. They frightened her with duppy stories at nights and could burst into songs which they all knew the words of – Jamaican folk songs at that, which her mother had forbidden her to sing because they were 'nigrish'.

In the daytime they wandered like a raucous flock all over the property and they knew the names of things and their uses: gully beans for stewing with saltfish, cerassie for bellyache. Every tree had a name, every bird in the sky (how did they *know* such things?), even the ants had names and personalities: red ants pepper ants black ants mad ants and pity-me-little. What a world where there were so many things to discover, even things that frightened her, for when she was with her mother, nothing was allowed to frighten her. How could these children know so much? And she so little! She was so ashamed of her ignorance. 'You don't know *anything*!' they cried day after day. They had to show her how to clean the lampshades with newspaper and trim the wicks, how to operate the bucket which got water from the tank, how to know by looking at the clouds whether there would be rain or fair weather, how to tell when soursop was ripe or pear about to drop from the tree. How to play hide-and-seek and really find a good hiding place when she was 'it'. How to make up and tell wonderful stories. How to be brave. And their games! Gigs they made themselves which spun, bright kites they glued together which actually flew, tough boys' games like 'Bull inna pen' in which she was always trampled, soft girls' games like 'Brown girl in the ring' and 'Jane and Louisa'.

Every year she felt ashamed to go to them with so little. And they had so much. She did have her beautiful clothes and shoes, her long plaits and bright ribbons and hair clips, her ring that her father had given her for her tenth birthday that had a real diamond, a fine watch that didn't need winding, and lots and lots of toys including a carousel that played a tune when you wound it with horses and riders that went round and round.

These things made her a hit with the cousins who eagerly awaited her coming so they could try on her beautiful clothes, wear her ring and admire her earrings in her newly pierced ears, and wind the carousel till it broke.

Despite their attentions she had the vague knowledge that they liked her not so much for herself as for the things that her parents had given her. Beside her cousins who were allowed to run wild and free, to shout, to quarrel and shriek, to laugh and sing — at least during the school holidays — she felt herself restricted, as if she were not a person in herself but a creation, an extension of her mother who even though she was not there was nevertheless a presence which she could not shake off long enough to express herself, to be. But she did not know what being herself meant, whether or not it wasn't simply a condition of making oneself liked by other people at whatever cost. So while the girl cousins played with her toys so much that she herself had no chance to even touch them, the boy cousins did dreadful things like hanging her dolls from trees and threatening to hang her too while she timidly smiled at them, her heart beating all the while. But smiling helped. She always smiled at everyone, even when she was frightened.

She loved best those late afternoons when her uncle would most courteously invite her for a walk. The other children snickered for they thought the uncle terribly old and boring. But she was too polite to refuse the first time he asked and after that, walking with her uncle became the highpoint of the holidays. The two of them would set off down the winding country road and he would greet each passerby as if he intimately knew them all. Best of all she liked it when he talked about the world they were passing through, noted the birds, told her their names and imitated their calls. With him she felt not frightened and threatened as she felt with the cousins but expansive as if her life was broadening, reaching out to touch the universe itself.

Sometimes he took her into the Chinese shop in the village square. He would seat her on top of a stack of full sugar bags near one end of the counter where she could see everything and drink a warm and sticky cream soda from the bottle (oh bliss!).

He would have a drink with the men who congregated at one end of the grocery counter which was tacitly understood to be the men's place. While he was chatting she had a chance to look around the shop, to absorb the sights, the smells, the way Mr Chin even while talking would dip up a little scoop of salt, flour or whatever and pour it onto a square of brown paper, deftly folding the paper into a cone ready for his customers who could afford to buy things only in small amounts.

She peeked into the barrels of salt herring and mackerel, loving their pungent smell which was totally foreign to her for such things were never eaten at home except by the maids and yard boys. At first she was scared of the shop, of the country people coming in and out, especially the women who wore pinafores which always smelled of the jackass rope which they carried in their pockets and smoked in their clay pipes and she was embarrased at first by the way everyone loudly admired her, exclaimed over her while the uncle proudly introduced her as his pretty little Kingston niece.

Whenever she went to the shop she became for a while the centre of everyone's good-humoured attention. At first she shrank away from these people surrounding her, for they were shoeless and coarse and black, and her mother was always warning her never to have anything to do with black people. But after a while she began to feel at ease in the warmth of the shop, in the way everybody knew everybody else and joked and chattered and hailed each other loudly. Under their attentions, their kindness which more and more extended to bits of sugar cane and paradise plum, mint balls and icy mints from Mr Chin's glass jars and (from Mr Chin himself) sweet-sour Chinese sweeties, she began to glow, to show off even, to chatter to them the way she never did to anyone else, to allow them to admire her earrings, her watch and her ring, her patent leather shoes with the straps, her skirt with the permanent pleats, feel her long curls, tie and untie her ribbons.

In the shop she felt happy as if there was nobody looking over her shoulder to see what she was doing. She knew that she would never tell her mother about the visits to Mr Chin's shop, for her mother said such places were dirty and smelly and overcharged because all Chinese were thieves, and her mother shopped only in the big supermarket with the shiny floors and silvery shopping carts where only people like herself shopped.

Every time she returned home, her mother got angry about a lot of things and said that it was the last time she would send her to the country for her sister took no care of her, look at her hair it was just like cane trash and full of knots and look at all the scratches and scabs on her knees and elbows and she hadn't cleaned out her ears once and had lost one foot off her good black patent leather shoes and had come back with nothing but mismatched socks, half of them didn't belong to her and was talking badly just like those country children. She was tired of correcting her and worst of all her skin was burnt black and it would take weeks and weeks to get her complexion fair and clear again.

Every year her mother threatened that she wouldn't send her back to the country. But the threat was never carried out, until one year when school ended, she announced that she was too big now to be going to the country and running wild and she would be taking her to Miami. After that she always spent her holidays in the States, sometimes with her mother but mostly on her own with her mother's relatives and friends in New York, Hartford, Houston, Los Angeles. Her mother always told them on the phone that she wanted Nolene to get some culture and she had her rounds of the movies, amusement parks and zoos. More and more her mother herself kept going to Miami, first on her endless buying trips, and then as she looked down the road and pronounced the island of her birth one with no future, she persuaded her husband to buy them a condo there. When Nolene left school it was inevitable that her mother would get her into a junior college in Miami where all the nice people's children went though it was costing them an arm and a leg to keep her there (her mother said). Nolene went through college the way she had gone through everything else, as in a dream, dutifully doing what her mother, her teachers told her, smiling always as in a dream, feeling that she had not yet entered into life, but was waiting.

Sitting in an office in Miami, playing at public relations, she continued to mark time, to be beautiful and sweet and good and not give her mother cause to be angry or disappointed in her. For she expressed her feelings in a shrill loud way that was frightening to Nolene since it contrasted so sharply with the genteel, ladylike tones her mother usually adopted otherwise.

When she met Philip she knew that this was what she had been waiting for. Of course the marriage, the meeting even, had all been arranged by her mother, for he was the son of a dear friend now living in Hartford. A fine young man, an economist with a Ph.D and prospects of becoming a university professor though she didn't like the idea of his going back to Jamaica to work, things were not looking so good down there and everybody knew that the university was a hotbed of communists. But they got married and went back (it was not so easy to get a university teaching job in the States) and Nolene's parents bought them the house as a wedding present.

Nolene was upset (though she didn't show it) that her mother was so insistent that the title should be in her name only. She was embarrassed but Philip laughed and shrugged it off. But it was just like her mother to spoil everything, to embarrass her with her coarseness, her loudness, her insistence on her 'rights' to the exclusion of everything else. Mother loved money, possessions, and was always giving Nolene lectures about how a woman should behave. Nolene knew that all the real estate they were acquiring in Miami was in her mother's name; her father didn't seem to care; he didn't seem to care about anything these days but getting out of the house and more and more spending his time at the Race Track. You see, her mother kept on saying, that's why you have to make sure that everything is in your name; you can't trust men not to throw it away overnight on the horses or kick you out for another woman. But, Nolene thought, these things are immaterial if you have love; she loved Philip so much she would have given him *everything*, only she realised she had nothing really to give.

At first it all went well. Philip was teaching at the university. The pay was poor but her mother helped them out from time to time with elaborate gifts and money regularly after the children arrived. Because they lived off the campus she hardly knew Philip's colleagues and having little to say, did not feel at home with those she did meet, since all they seemed to do was talk and argue. More and more her world became that of home and children, for after Tracey-Ann was born Philip refused to let her work again. A mother's place, he said, is at home with her young children and she wondered how he could claim to be so 'progressive' yet be so old-fashioned about these things. She did not want to stay home, she liked going out to work, she liked getting up in the mornings and getting dressed, driving in rush hour traffic, functioning at a job, for these things made her feel good about herself, capable and wanted, in touch with a vibrant world of her own out there. But she stayed at home as Philip wanted because she knew that this was what would please him best.

But things, the country, started to change around them; they installed burglar bars on all the windows (paid for by her mother), and now she drove with her car windows up all the time. The women who phoned each other now talked of nothing but shortages in the supermarket and the latest horrors of who had been raped last night. And the trickle to Miami turned into a flood.

Everyone was caught up in politics. Philip too. He had begun to make a name for himself off campus by writing articles for the Sunday papers analysing the economy and people started to sit up and take notice. He was one of the few university men who bothered to get off the campus and out into the community, they said, and what is more, he was not scruffy like the rest of them in their beards and sandals. He had leftist leanings, it is true, but was no Communist agitator, and the Rotary Club, the Chamber of Commerce, the Jaycees and even the Soroptimists felt safe enough to invite him to address them. More than that, the businessmen were beginning to overcome their distrust of the university, of men of learning, and were embracing those who called themselves consultants, as Philip came to be. This, along with what Nolene's mother sent, helped to pay for the Volvo which he had just acquired, for his PC, the video, the badminton court and an apartment on the north coast. He was also beginning to get a rush from the politicians, both parties recognising that any specialist in international monetary studies was one of the bright boys to watch.

But Philip could see where the wind was blowing and threw in his lot with the PNP, and when that party came to power in their massive landslide victory, he was one of the three or four bright university types who became the Prime Minister's chief advisers.

Life changed for them then; she saw less and less of him; sometimes he didn't come home for days at a time or else their house was turned into an extension of Jamaica House, with people coming and going at all hours while they worked on the Plan. She never knew what Plan, if it was one that kept changing, or many. All she knew was that this was the time that Philip began to openly express his dissatisfaction with her – he kept urging her to do something, get committed, get involved in the work of the Party, in the women's movement. And though she dutifully tried, she was put off by these brilliant women suddenly out there who were talking their heads off, taking to the platforms, chopping off their hair into low Afros or wearing head wraps, making strident and positive noises.

Most of all she was frightened by Philip's PA – his personal assistant. All the clever young men had one in those days – young women who were bright, efficient, bursting with commitment and politically unimpeachable. Philip's PA was Jennifer, a short, stout very black girl whose Afro hair style made her look mannish, but who had the most devastating smile and apparently a limitless fund of energy since she was on call twenty-four hours a day. Jennifer drank and smoked and swore, was loud and argumentative and could hold her own with the best of the men, the kind of woman Nolene had been taught to dislike, the kind of woman who in the early days of their marriage Philip had expressed contempt for. Now whenever

Jennifer or any of the party women came to the house she locked herself into her bedroom and sat on the verandah watching the birds. The men were more bearable, they were men after all and she was an attractive woman; it was the women who scared her, made her feel inept and silly. Nowadays, especially, she knew they were particularly critical of women like her, women who still wore their nails long and polished, who still went dressed up to the supermarket, creamed their hair and refused to wrap their heads, women who worried about irrelevances like corn-flakes and toys. It was not that she was being defiant in running against the tide, it was simply that it was easier for her to continue to be the kind of person her mother had brought her up to be than to go with the now popular style.

Philip for all his involvement with the party also had his eyes down the road and it was he who decided that, for safety's sake, she and the children should go to live abroad. She didn't want to leave him, hated Miami and dreaded being again under her mother's thumb. But what weapons did she have to fight with? She ended up going.

The news from home got worse and worse and she worried about Philip but she saw him often, if only for the brief stopover he contrived through Miami on his many official trips abroad. Before he arrived he usually called her with a long shopping list of things which he needed and couldn't get at home. He always went home laden with bags of detergent, rice, car parts, whisky, as did everyone else. At first she didn't mind shopping for Philip – with her money. She knew he had no foreign exchange and felt proud after all these years to be contributing something. She didn't mind at first when he called asking her to send him money at some stop along the way. But his demands got more and more frequent for larger and larger sums and she found that the time came when all her savings were depleted and she was trying harder and harder to make ends meet. More and more she began to resent the fact that she was being taken for granted, for the minute he had put her on a plane for Miami he had absolved himself of all responsibility for her and the children. After all it was impossible to get money out of Jamaica and in any case the situation was only temporary; so he didn't know how she schooled and fed the children and paid the rent. But it was now two years and he had used up all her money.

All of these thoughts remained unspoken even when her financial situation became so critical she began to live on loans. But she never really got angry until she discovered that a great deal of what she bought for her husband was in fact intended for his friends and political colleagues, and the money she sent to different parts of the world was sometimes for others. Though she had never lost her temper in her life, it made her unbearably angry when he phoned and asked her to buy two car tyres that she knew were not his car size and turned so waspish when she told him she did not have the money to do so. He was shouting over the phone that she was embarrassing him in front of his friends since he had assured them that he could get the tyres and if she couldn't pick up one or two things for him in Miami from time to time, what good was she? She in turn had got angry, for the first time in their married life had dared to differ, and he was speechless on the long distance line as she poured out her grievances, her anxieties, all that had been bottled up these years: her loneliness, her fears of what the children were learning in Miami, how she could no longer control them, they no longer listened to her, how he put his friends, his political career before their welfare. But by that time he had stopped listening. Appalled at what she had done she tried to call him back but his line rang for a day and a night without answer and when she got his office his PA – the same one, Jennifer – claimed that he was away on 'retreat' and she would have him call her sometime. Sometime? How dare she? How dare this woman tell her such a thing. About her husband. How dare he go off without leaving a number where he could be reached. Suppose there was an emergency with one of the children? She cried herself to sleep. But she woke up feeling not saddened, but defiant, as if she had already crossed a bridge when she had argued with Philip and had to continue down that road.

Lying in bed she thought for the first time in years of the bird tree, of the foolish kling-klings and the faithful domesticated pecharies, of the concerts by the mockingbirds and the sweet calls of the john chewitts in April, felt an unbearable longing to go home, to see her husband, to talk to him, to tell him that she couldn't live in a place without real trees, without birds, that she didn't want her children to grow up not knowing how to cast spells on lizards so they'd stand still, make fee-fees out of flowers and know cerassie bush for bellyache. And the thought of the pecharies inspired her: why couldn't she be a pechary and defend her territory, chase out the foolish kling-klings – like Jennifer. Just like that, she decided to go home. Doing each thing she had never dared to do before gave her a new elation as if she were discovering a world out there where all things had names and everything had a purpose and she was not so ignorant and foolish after all.

She bought a ticket without telling anyone, not even her mother, in fact lied to her mother, telling her that Philip had asked her to come home for a few days. Her mother took the children and she got on a plane; she decided not to tell Philip she was coming; she would take a taxi in from the airport and surprise him.

But when she got home – strange to call it that – no one was there except a new helper who looked at her wildly when she announced who she was. She couldn't understand why the woman's eyes bulged as if she were seeing a duppy. As she walked into the house, the helper moved as if to block her way but she ignored the woman and noted with some surprise that the living room furniture had been completely rearranged and there were fresh flowers all around. In the master bedroom she threw open the French windows that led to the verandah and went out to take a deep breath of the fresh air, her eyes immediately falling on the bird tree. And though she listened and strained her eyes she could see no sign of birds. But not for long. Soon the garden was filled with the unmistakably raucous sounds of the kling-klings and when the flock crossed into the garden and settled in the topmost branches of the tree, she knew that it was not pechary season. She watched the kling-klings for a while and then turned inside. As her eyes became accustomed to the darkened room she noted the easy chair in the corner on which reposed a woman's slip, neatly folded. And as she took in carefully the rest of the room, she saw women's clothes in the closet that were not hers, perfume bottles on her dressing table, someone else's underwear in her chest of drawers, someone else's jewellery, someone's scent.

The frightened helper who had been watching her from the doorway now fled as if she were to be personally held responsible for the disaster about to overtake the house. She must have telephoned Philip for he arrived soon after and showed no surprise to see her and – she was glad of it – made no attempt to dissemble. He came straight to the point at once though she thought that for a university lecturer he was unbearably rambling thereafter:

'Nolene I am sorry that I did not tell you. You had to come and find out, but if you had told me you were coming I would have met you. What did you expect me to do? You went off to Miami and left me here alone a man of flesh and blood. Never interested in my work the party comrades Jennifer.'

Jennifer? Nolene till that moment was barely listening to what he was saying, her mind too numb to really take it in. But Jennifer? A kling-kling? She giggled hysterically.

'Well, you know we have been working closely together. You and I never had anything in common really. You never tried. Just like your mother all you are interested in is acquiring things . . . status . . . money . . . materialism . . . class interest . . . bourgeoisie.'

She was now only hearing fragments of his talk. Oh God, she thought. She never knew it would be like this. She thought he would at least have had something to say to her, about their marriage, about being sorry, about asking her to forgive him, but he was talking about:

'Jennifer . . . the society . . . struggle and I feel the best thing would be for you to go back to Miami as soon as possible.

Now that you know I'll file for divorce. Jack will handle it. Desertion, no problem. It's almost three years. I know you won't want to contest it. You can have the children. I won't contest that either. I know you will never come back to Jamaica to live. Commitment . . . struggle. If you give me your ticket I will get you on the first plane out tomorrow. I know it's a shock but it's probably best that you find out like this so I don't have to spell anything out for you.'

She didn't know when he left after giving up trying to get her to speak to him and she didn't know what time she fell asleep, in the children's room. At least no one had taken that over. It was the same as they had left it, with their tattered books, their old toys, their crayon drawings on the walls. Her last thoughts before she fell asleep in a small bed was that it made her sad to see the remnants of what they had been for they had grown so much in the last two years, beyond her, beyond their years. Now they would never know about the birds or the names of bushes and trees and what to cry to keep wasps away. For when she left in the morning she would never have any reason to come back to Jamaica.

Next morning she still felt confused and bewildered and Philip was nowhere to be seen; she didn't know if he had even spent the night there. She woke at dawn and did what she had always done, went out on to the verandah. And, as if they had been waiting for her, she was immediately treated to a concert by the mockingbirds; three of them that took it in turn to sing their rapture from an electric light pole, treetop and verandah railing. The mockingbirds always amused her, straining with their small bodies for notes almost beyond their grasp, such complicated songs of rapture, pouring out sound after sound. Standing on the verandah she listened, startled, confused, having forgotten what it was like to hear mockingbirds in the morning.

The mockingbirds awakened something in her that harkened back to her childhood, to the time with the country cousins when she had first had a sense of being nobody, and an anger started to build up inside her, anger at her mother who had claimed her life as her own and shifted her around and then handed her over to another; at Philip who had taken her over, who had shifted her around and was now handing her back to her mother. And who was she now? And had she ever been anyone? And who were they to determine her life so? Even the birds – the pecharies, the kling-klings, the mockingbirds – knew clearly who they were, had established their own territory, their own hierarchy, their own notions of family life.

And this house of humans now was no better than the bird tree for Philip had turned it into a tenantry – one bird out, another in.

She sat there thinking for a long long time, getting angrier and angrier, her very anger hardening her, dragging her away from the tree, from the birds, forcing her to focus on her very self. *This* woman sitting alone on *this* verandah now. And finally she came to her decision. She thought, to hell with it! She would throw out the crotons and the anthuriums, the gerberas and the ixorias. She would plant a new garden. First, she would find the gardener and tell him never to touch the bird tree. It was *her* tree and *her* house and she was staying. *He* could move out.

Just to make sure she cried: 'Green Bush. Green Bush. Green Bush.' Laughing at the craziness of it. The power.

The Two Grandmothers

I

MUMMY, you know what? Grandma Del has baby chickens.
Yellow and white ones. She made me hold them. And I help
her gather eggs but I don't like to go out the back alone because
the turkey gobbler goes gobble! gobble! gobble! after my legs,
he scares me, and Mr SonSon next door has baby pigs I don't
like the mother pig though. Grandma lives in this pretty little
house with white lace curtains at all the windows, Mummy you
must come with me and Daddy next time, and you can peek
through the louvres Grandma calls them jalousies isn't that
funny and you can see the people passing by. But they can't see
you. Mummy why can't we have lace curtains like Grandma
Del so we can peek through nobody ever goes by our house
except the gardeners and the maids and people begging and
Rastas selling brooms? Many many people go by Grandma
Del's house they all call out to her and Grandma Del knows
everyone. My special friend is Miss Princess the postmistress
who plays the organ in church she wears tight shiny dresses and
her hair piled *so* on her head and she walks *very slow* and everybody says she is sweet on Mister Blake who is the new teacher
and he takes the service in church when Parson doesn't come
and then Miss Princess gets so nervous she mixes up all the
hymns. Mister Mack came to fix Grandma's roof and Grandma
said 'poorman poorman' all the time. Mister Mack's daughters
Eulalie and Ermandine are big girls at high school in town
though Eulalie fell and they don't know what is to be done.

62

Mummy, why are they so worried that Eulalie fell? She didn't break her leg or anything for she is walking up and down past the house all day long and looks perfectly fine to me.

Mummy, I really like Grandma Del's house it's nice and cosy and dark and cool inside with these lovely big picture frames of her family and Daddy as a baby and Daddy as a little boy and Daddy on the high school football team, they won Manning Cup that year Grandma says, did you know that Mummy? and Daddy at University and a wedding picture of Daddy and you and me as a baby and all the pictures you send Grandma every year but those are the small pictures on the side table with the lovely white lace tablecloth. In the picture frame on the wall there is Great-grandpapa Del with a long beard and whiskers, he is sitting down in a chair and Great-grandmama is standing behind him, and then there is a picture of Grandma herself as a young lady with her hair piled high like Miss Princess and her legs crossed at the ankles she looks so lovely. But you know what, Mummy, I didn't see a picture of Daddy's father and when I asked Grandma she got mad and shooed me away. She got even madder when I asked her to show me her wedding picture. I only wanted to see it.

Mummy, do you know that Grandma sends me to Sunday School? We stay over for big church and I walk home with her and all the people, it's so nice. Only Parson comes to church in a car. Mummy did you go to Sunday School? I go with Joycie a big girl next door and Grandma made me three dresses to wear. She says she cannot imagine how a girl-child (that's me) can leave home with nothing but blue jeans and T-shirts and shorts and not a single church dress. She has this funny sewing machine, not like Aunt Thelma's, she has to use her feet to make it go just like the organ in church Miss Princess pumps away with her feet to make it give out this lovely sound and works so hard you should see her and the first time I went to Grandma's church I was so scared of the bats! The church is full of bats but usually they stay high up in the roof. But as soon as the organ starts playing on Sunday the bats start swooping lower and lower and one swooped so low I nearly died of fright and clutched Grandma Del so tight my hat flew off.

Did I tell you Grandma made me a hat to wear to church with her own two hands? She pulled apart one of her old straw hats, leghorn she said, and made me a little hat that fits just so on my head with a bunch of tiny pink flowers. Grandma didn't send it with me though, or my Sunday dresses, she says she will keep them till I return for she knows that I am growing heathenish in town. When Grandma dresses me up for church I feel so beautiful in my dresses she made with lace and bows and little tucks so beautiful and my hat, I feel so special that my own Grandma made these for me with her own two hands and didn't buy them in a store. Grandma loves to comb my hair she says it's so long and thick and she rubs it with castor oil every night. I hate the smell of castor oil but she says it's the best thing for hair and after a time I even like the smell. Grandma Del says my skin is beautiful like honey and all in all I am a fine brown lady and must make sure to grow as beautiful inside as I am outside but Mummy, how do I go about doing that?

Nights at Grandma are very funny. Mummy can you imagine there's no TV? And its very, very dark. No street lights or any lights. We go to bed early and every night Grandma lights the oil lamps and then we blow them out when we are going to bed, you have to take a deep breath, and every morning Grandma checks the oil in the lamps and cleans the shades. They have 'Home Sweet Home' written all around them. So beautiful. She cleans the shades with newspapers. She says when I come next year I'll be old enough to clean them all by myself. Grandma knows such lovely stories; she tells me stories every night not stories from a book you know, Mummy, the way you read to me, but stories straight from her head. Really! I am going to learn stories from Grandma so when I am a grown lady I will remember all these stories to tell my children. Mummy, do you think I will?

II

Mummy, you know Grandma Elaine is so funny she says I'm
not to call her Grandma any more, I'm to call her Towser like
everybody else for I'm growing so fast nobody would believe
that she could have such a big young lady for a granddaughter.
I think it's funny I'm practising calling her Towser though she
is still my grandmother. I said to her, 'Grandmother, I mean
Towser, Grandma Del introduces me to everyone as her granddaughter she calls me her "little gran".' And Grandma Elaine
says, 'Darling, the way your Grandmother Del looks and
conducts herself she couldn't be anything but a grandmother
and honey she and I are of entirely different generations.'

Grandma Elaine says such funny things sometimes. Like she
was dressing to go out last night and she was putting on make
up and I said 'Grandma' (she was still Grandma then) I said,
'Grandma, you shouldn't paint your face like that you know,
it is written in the Bible that it's a sin. Grandma Del says so
and I will never paint my face.' And she said, 'Darling, with
all due respect to your paternal grandmother, she's a lovely lady
or was when I met her the one and only time at the wedding,
and she has done one absolutely fantastic thing in her life which
is to produce one son your esteemed father, one hunk of a guy,
but honey, other than that your Grandmother Del is a country
bumpkin of the deepest waters and don't quote her goddam
sayings to me.' Mummy, you know Grandma Elaine *swears* like
that all the time? I said, 'Grandma you mustn't swear and take
the name of the Lord in vain.' And she said, 'Honeychile with
all due respect to the grey hairs of your old grandmother and
the first class brainwashing your daddy is allowing her to give
you, I wish my granddaughter would get off my back and leave
me to go to Hell in peace.' Can you imagine she said that?

She's really mad that you allow me to spend time with
Grandma Del. She says, 'Honey, I really don't know what your
mother thinks she is doing making you spend so much time
down there in the deepest darkest country. I really must take
you in hand. It's embarrassing to hear some of the things you

come out with sometimes. Your mother would be better advised to send you to Charm School next summer you are never too young to start. Melody-Ann next door went last year and it's done wonders for her, turned her from a tomboy into a real little lady.' (Though Mummy, I really can't stand Melody-Ann any more, you know.) 'And your mother had better start to do something about your hair from now it's almost as tough as your father's and I warned your mother about it from the very start I said "Honey, love's alright but what about the children's hair?". If you were my child I would cut it right off to get some of the kinks out.' Mummy, you won't cut off my hair, will you? Daddy and Grandma Del like it just the way it is. What does Grandma Elaine mean when she says my hair is tough, Mummy?

Anyway, Mummy, can I tell you a secret? Gran, I mean Towser, told me and says it's a secret but I guess since you are her daughter she won't mind if I tell you. Do you know that Towser has a new boyfriend? He came to pick her up on Saturday night, remember I told you Joyce was staying up with me and we watched TV together while Towser went out? That's the time she was painting her face and she put on her fabulous silver evening dress, you know the strapless one and her diamonds with it, the ones her husband after Grandpapa gave her, and I was so proud she was my grandmama she looked wonderful like a million dollars and when I told her so she let me spray some of her perfume on myself before Mister Kincaid came. He is a tall white man and he kissed Towser's hand and then he kissed my hand and he had a drink with Towser and was very nice and they drove off in a big white car like what Uncle Frank drives Mummy, a Benz, and Towser was looking so pleased the whole time, and before Mister Kincaid came she whispered and said her new boyfriend was coming to take her to dinner and he was so nice and handsome and rich. Towser was looking as pleased as Eulalie did when the mail van driver was touching her when they thought nobody was looking but I was peeking through the louvres at Grandma Del's and I saw them.

But Mummy, I don't know why Towser wants me to spend more time with her for she is never there when I go; always rushing off to the gym and the pool and dinners and cocktails or else she is on the phone. I love Towser so much though, she hugs me a lot and says things that make me laugh and she gives me wonderful presents. Do you know she made Joyce bake a chocolate cake for me? And my new bracelet is so lovely. It's my birthstone you know, Mummy. You know what, Grandma Elaine, I mean Towser, says she is going to talk to you about taking me to see my cousins Jason and Maureen in Clearwater when she goes to do her Christmas shopping in Miami. Oh Mummy, can I go? You know all the girls in my class have been to Miami and you've never taken me. Mum, can we go to Disneyworld soon? I'm so ashamed everyone in school has been to Disneyworld and I haven't gone yet. When Towser goes out Joyce and I sit in the den and watch TV the whole time, except I usually fall asleep during the late show but Joyce watches everything until TV signs off, and next morning when she is making me breakfast she tells me all the parts that I missed. Mummy, can't we get a video? Everyone in my class has a video at home except me. You know Towser is getting a video she says she is getting Mister Kincaid to give her one as a present. Towser is so much fun. Except, Mummy, what does she have against my hair? And my skin? She always seems angry about it and Joyce says Grandma is sorry I came out dark because she is almost a white lady and I am really dark. But Mummy, what is wrong with that? When I hold my hand next to Joyce my skin is not as dark as hers or Grandma Del's or Daddy's even. Is dark really bad, Mummy?

III

Mummy, did you know that a whistling woman and a crowing hen are an abomination to the Lord? That's what Grandma Del told me and Pearlie when Pearlie was teaching me to whistle. Don't tell Grandma but I *can* whistle. Want to hear me? –! –!

–! Ha ha. Mummy, can you whistle? Pearlie is my best friend in the country, she lives near to Grandma in this tiny house, so many of them and all the children sleep together in one room on the floor and Mummy, you know what? Pearlie has only one pair of shoes and one good dress and her school uniform though she hardly goes to school and some old things she wears around the house that have holes in them. Can you imagine? And you should see her little brothers! Half the time they are wearing no clothes at all. Mummy, can you send Pearlie some of my dresses and some of my toys but not my Barbie doll? She doesn't have any toys at all, not a single one.

And Pearlie is just a little older than me and she has to look after her little brothers when her Mummy goes to work. She has to feed them and bathe them and change them and while she is changing the baby's nappies her little brothers get into so much trouble. And when they break things when her mother comes home she beats Pearlie. Poor Pearlie! She can balance a pan of water on her head no hands you know. I wish I could do that. She goes to the standpipe for water and carries the pan on her head without spilling a drop. Sometimes I go with her; I borrow a pan and though it's smaller than Pearlie's I always end up spilling the water all over me and the pan gets heavier and heavier till I can hardly bear it before we get to Pearlie's house. Pearlie can wash clothes too. I mean real clothes, not dolly clothes. Really. Her baby brother's nappies and things and she cooks dinner for them but the way they eat is really funny. They don't have a real kitchen or anything. She has three big rocks in the fireplace and she catches up a fire when she is ready and she has to fan it and fan it with an old basket top and there is a lot of smoke. It makes me sneeze. Then when the fire is going she puts on a big pot of water and when it is boiling she peels things and throws them in the water to cook – yams and cocos and green bananas and that's what they eat, no meat or rice or salad or anything. Pearlie uses a sharp knife just like a big person and she peels the bananas ever so fast, she makes three cuts and goes zip! zip! with her fingers and the banana is out of its skin and into the pot. She says you must never put bananas and yams to boil in cold water for they will get drunk and never cook. Did you know that?

Once I helped her to rub up the flour dumplings but my dumplings came out so soft Pearlie said they were like fla-fla and she won't let me help her make dumplings again. Pearlie has to do all these things and we only get to play in the evenings when her mother comes home and can you imagine, Mummy, Pearlie has never seen TV? And she has never been to the movies. Never. Mummy, do you think Pearlie could come and live with us? I could take her to the movies though I don't know who would look after her baby brothers when her mother goes to work. You know Pearlie doesn't have a father? She doesn't know where he is. I'd die without my Daddy. Grandma Del says I'm to be careful and not spend so much time with Pearlie for Pearlie is beginning to back-chat and is getting very force-ripe. Mummy, what is force-ripe?

Sometimes I play with Eulalie's baby. His name is Oral and he is fat and happy and I help to change his nappy. He likes me a lot and claps his hands when he sees me and he has two teeth already. He likes to grab hold of my hair and we have a hard time getting him to let go. Mummy why can't I have a baby brother to play with all the time? Eulalie and Ermandine love to comb my hair and play with it they say I am lucky to have tall hair but Grandma Del doesn't like Eulalie and Ermandine any more. She says they are a disgraceful Jezebel-lot and dry-eye and bring down shame on their father and mother who try so hard with them. Sometimes my Grandma talks like that and I really don't understand and when I ask her to explain she says, 'Cockroach nuh bizniz inna fowl roos,' and she acts real mad as if I did something wrong and I don't know why she is so vexed sometimes and quarrels with everyone even me. She scares me when she is vexed.

You know when Grandma Del is really happy? When she is baking cakes and making pimento liqueur and orange marmalade and guava jelly. Oh, she sings and gets Emmanuel to make up a big fire out in the yard and they put on this big big pot and we peel and we peel guava – hundreds of them. When we make stewed guavas she gives me a little spoon so I can help to scoop out the seeds and I have to be real careful to do it properly and not break the shells. Mummy, right here you have this little glass jar full of stewed guavas from Grandma Del that I helped to make. Grandma gets so happy to see her kitchen full of these lovely glass jars full of marmalade and guava jelly. But you know what? Grandma just makes it and then she gives it all away. Isn't that funny? And one time she baked a wedding cake and decorated it too – three cakes in different sizes she made and then she put them one on top of the other. Grandma is so clever. She allowed me to help her stir the cake mix in the bowl but it was so heavy I could barely move the spoon. When it was all finished she let me use my fingers to lick out the mixing bowls. Yum Yum. Why don't you bake cakes so I can lick out the bowls, Mummy?

This time I found that I had grown so much I couldn't get into the church dresses Grandma made for me last time. So she made me some new dresses and she says she will give the old ones to Pearlie. Mummy can you believe that everyone in church remembered me? And they said: 'WAT-A-WAY-YU-GROW' and 'HOW-IS-YU-DAADIE?' and 'HOW-IS-YU-MAAMIE?' till I was tired. Mummy, that is the way they talk, you know, just like Richie and the gardener next door. 'WAT-A-WAY-YU-GROW.' They don't speak properly the way we do, you know. Mummy, Eulalie and Ermandine don't go to church or school anymore and Ermandine says when I come back next year she will have a little baby for me to play with too and Eulalie says *she* will have a new little baby.

IV

MUMMY, you know what the girls in school say? They say I am the prettiest girl in school and I can be Miss Jamaica. When I'm big I'll go to the gym like you so I can keep my figure and I must take care of my skin for even though I have excellent skin, Towser says, I must always care for it. Towser spends hours before the mirror every morning caring for her skin and her new boyfriend Mister Samuels is always telling her how beautiful she looks. Towser really loves that. Mister Samuels is taking her to Mexico for the long Easter weekend and Towser is going to Miami to buy a whole new wardrobe for the trip. She says she is going to bring me all the new movies for the video. Mummy, when I am old like Grandma will men tell me I'm beautiful too? Can I have my hair relaxed as soon as I am twelve as you promised? Will you allow me to enter Miss Jamaica when I am old enough? You know Jason likes me a lot but he's my cousin so he doesn't count. Mom, am I going to Clearwater again this Christmas to spend time with Jason and Maureen? Maureen is always fighting with me you know but Jason says she's jealous because she isn't pretty like me, she's fat and she has to wear braces on her teeth. Will I ever have to wear braces? Mom, when I go to Miami can I get a training bra? All the girls in my class are wearing them and a make up starter kit? Mom, when are we going to get a Dish?

V

Mom, do I have to go Grandma Del's again? It's so boring. There's nothing to do and nobody to talk to and I'm ashamed when my friends ask me where I'm going for the holidays and I have to tell them only to my old grandmother in the country. You know Gina is going to Europe and Melody-Ann is spending all of her holidays in California and Jean-Ann is going to her aunt in Trinidad? Mom, even though Grandma Del has electricity now she has only a small black and white TV, and I end up missing everything for she doesn't want me to watch the late show even on weekends, and Grandma's house is so small and crowded and dark and she goes around turning off lights and at nights Grandma smells because she is always rubbing herself with liniment for her arthritis and it's true Grandma is in terrible pain sometimes. Mummy what is going to happen to Grandma when she is real old? She's all alone there.

She got mad at me when I told her I didn't want her to rub

castor oil in my hair anymore because I was having it conditioned and the castor oil smells so awful. And on Sundays Grandma still wants me to go to church with her. It's so boring. We have to *walk* to church and back. It's *miles* in the hot sun. I can't walk on the gravel road in my heels. If a parent passed and saw me there among all the country bumpkin I would die and Grandma says I am far too young to be wearing heels even little ones and I tell Grandma I'm not young any more. I'll be entering high school next term and everybody is wearing heels. She criticises everything I do as if I am still a baby and she doesn't like me wearing lip gloss or blusher though I tell her you allow me to wear them. And Grandma still wants me to come and greet all her friends, it's so boring as soon as somebody comes to the house she calls me and I have to drop whatever I am doing, even watching TV, and I have to say hello to all these stupid people. It's so boring Mom you wouldn't believe it, there's nobody but black people where Grandma lives and they don't know anything, they ask such silly questions. And they are dirty. You know this girl Pearlie I used to play with when I was little she is so awful-looking, going on the road with her clothes all torn up and you should see her little brothers always dirty and in rags with their noses running. I can't stand to have them around me and Pearlie and everybody is always begging me clothes and things and I can't stand it so I don't even bother to go outside the house half the time. When anybody comes I can see them through the louvres and I just pretend I am not there or I am sleeping. And everybody is just having babies without being married like Pearlie's mother and they are not ashamed. The worst ones are those two sisters Eulalie and Ermandine, you can't imagine how many children they have between them a new one every year and Grandma says not a man to mind them.

But Mummy, something terrible happened. That Eulalie and I got into an argument. She's so ignorant and I told her it was a disgrace to have babies without being married and she said, 'Who says?' and I said, 'Everybody. My Mummy and Grandma Elaine and Grandma Del for a start.' And she said, 'Grandma

Del? Yes? You ever hear that she that is without sin must cast
the first stone?' And I said, 'What do you mean?' And she said,
'Ask your Grannie Del Miss High-And-Mighty since her son
turn big-shot and all. Ask her who his father? And why she
never turn teacher? And why her daddy almost turn her out of
the house and never speak to her for five years? And why they
take so long to let her into Mothers Union?' And Eulalie
wouldn't tell me anymore and they were so awful to me, they
started singing, 'Before A married an' go hug up mango tree,
A wi' live so. Me one.' You know that song, Mummy? I went
home to ask Grandma Del what Eulalie meant but Mummy
when I got home it was just weird I got so scared that I got
this terrible pain in my tummy, my tummy hurt so much I
couldn't ask Grandma Del anything and then when I felt better,
I couldn't bring myself to say anything for I'm scared Grandma
Del will get mad. But Mummy, do you think Grandma Del had
Daddy without getting married? Is that what Eulalie meant?
Mummy, wouldn't that make Daddy a bastard?

VI

Mummy, please don't send me to stay with Auntie Rita in
Clearwater again. Ever. Nothing, Mummy. . . . . It's that
Maureen. She doesn't like me.

. . . .

Mummy, am I really a nigger? That's what Maureen said when
we were playing one day and she got mad at me and she said,
'You're only a goddam nigger you don't know any better.
Auntie Evie married a big black man and you're his child and
you're not fit to play with me.' Mummy, I gave her such a box
that she fell and I didn't care. I cried and cried and though
Auntie Rita spanked Maureen afterwards and sent her to bed
without any supper, I couldn't eat my supper for I had this pain
in my tummy, such a terrible pain and Uncle Rob came into
the bedroom and held my hand and said that Maureen was a

naughty girl and he was ashamed of her and *he* thought I was a very beautiful, lovely girl. . . . .

But Mummy, how can I be beautiful? My skin is so dark, darker than yours and Maureen's and Jason's and Auntie Rita's. And my hair is so coarse, not like yours or Maureen's but then Maureen's father is white. Is that why Maureen called me a nigger? I hate Maureen. She is fat and ugly and still wearing braces. . . . .

. . . .

Mummy, why can't I have straight hair like Maureen? I'm so ashamed of my hair. I simply can't go back to Clearwater.

VII

Mom, I don't care what Dad says I can't go to stay with Grandma Del this summer because the Charm Course is for three weeks and then remember Towser is taking me to Ochi for three weeks in her new cottage. Do you think Towser is going to marry Mr Blake? Then I am going with you to Atlanta. You promised. So I really don't have any time to spend with Grandma this summer. And next holidays remember you said I can go to Venezuela on the school trip? I don't know what Dad is on about because if he feels so strongly why doesn't he go and spend time with his mother? Only that's a laugh because Daddy doesn't have time for anybody any more, I mean is there ever a time nowadays when he is at home? I know Grandma Del is getting old and she is all alone but she won't miss me, she quarrels with me all the time I am there. Mom, I just can't fit her in and that is that.

. . . .

O.K. You know what? I have an idea. Why don't we just take a quick run down to see Grandma this Sunday and then we won't have to worry about her again till next year? Daddy can take us and we can leave here real early in the morning though

I don't know how I am going to get up early after Melody-Ann's birthday party Saturday night, but we don't have too stay long with Grandma Del. We can leave there right after lunch so we will be back home in time to watch *Dallas*. Eh, Mom?

Tears of the Sea

SHE never knew why the load of sand with the shells had been brought there in the first place, all she could remember was the excitement of its arrival: the truck huffing over the hill and belching smoke, the rush to open the gate, the backing up and to-and-froing, the revving of the engine, everyone gathered round for the moment when the back of the truck was finally in line with the top barbecue, the gate opened and the gleaming load of sand was shovelled out. Even before the sand stopped falling from the truck she found herself in it and everyone laughed; she was laughing herself, jumping up and down in the sand, fully dressed, believing that it had been brought all the way from the seashore especially for her.

Usually the barbecues had no space for anything as frivolous as sand. The barbecues were constantly in use for drying things – pimento and corn, cocoa and coffee and ginger. But now perhaps everything was out of season for the barbecues were empty except for the one truck load of sand. And this sand was white and gleaming and different from the black river sand which was all she was used to, for she had never been to the seashore.

But she had often seen the sea as the car rounded a bend in the hill which overlooked the town, for a moment glimpsed from afar as part of a world split in three – the sky, the land, and the sea. The sea was always changeable, always surprising: sometimes indigo, sometimes pale green, sometimes emerald, sometimes indistinguishable from the sky itself when it was grey and threatening. And where the sea hit the shore there was a constant band of gleaming white which, Grandma said, were beaches. The sea in her imagination was something that was constantly alive, constantly changing and, though she could hear no sounds from afar, constantly roaring. But the sea she had never seen up close for once they got off the hill and into the town which was hot and sticky and crowded and noisy, they could no longer see anything but the streets, the houses, could no longer imagine even that something as remarkable as the sea was a living, breathing thing so close to them just beyond the tops of the houses. More than anything else she yearned to see the sea real close, to walk on the beach, to watch the breakers surge. But Grandma had instantly dismissed her wish to go to the seaside as something impossible. 'Do you imagine we are tourists?' she said, and though she didn't explain what those were, they were not, she implied, good solid people like themselves. But that didn't stifle her yearning, only smouldered her desire to see the sea, walk on the sands, even once, although she never voiced the desire again. And now here was sand from that sea, white and gleaming, full, she discovered almost immediately, of tiny shells.

Now she spent all her time in the sand pile on the barbecue, pushing deeper and deeper down to watch the sand grains fall, lying down and completely covering herself in the hot sand which rocked her in its cradle until she almost fell asleep. Sometimes when she was lying in the sand and was perfectly relaxed she would feel softly at first, then stronger, a breeze which she knew was coming directly from the sea and she heard in its wake the faint roar, the sound of the sea coming all the way from the coast to where she lay on a barbecue on a mountain top.

And she played games with the shells. She lined them up on the ledge of the barbecue according to shape, to colour, then in order of size. She became a general and they her army, a schoolteacher and they her pupils, a mother and they her numerous children. Each day she found more and more shells as if they were as endless as the sand grains, bits and pieces of shell, of coral and seafans. And one day she found *the* shell. It was the only one of its kind in the sandpile, in the whole world, she thought, almost a replica of the giant conch shells in the garden, but so tiny that it fitted in the palm of her hand and unlike the big conch shells that were bleached white and looked old and worn, this little shell was new and inviting, its deep interior shading to a salmon colour lustre with a touch of mother-of-pearl, its outside ranging from the most delicate pink to gleaming white. It was the most beautiful thing she had ever seen. She immediately knew that it was a magic shell sent specially to her as a gift from the sea, and so she was not surprised one day when she held it to her ear to hear first the faint but familiar roar of the ocean and then coming scratchily at first, like the radio, a voice from afar. 'Hello', it said. 'Hello. Hello'. And she finally answered breathless and timid, 'Hello'.

But after their initial shyness the shell and she became good friends. They held long conversations on many subjects but mostly about the sea and the creatures that lived there, of seashells and seaweed, for she had an intense curiosity about the sea. 'Why don't you go and see for yourself,' the shell had asked her.

'Because I have nobody to take me,' she replied. So the sea shell told her as much as she could about the sea.

'We sea shells,' the sea shell said, 'are the tears of the sea.'

'But why does the sea cry so much?' she couldn't help asking.

'Because it needs a lot of water. Otherwise it would run dry.'

'Oh.' The sea shell seemed so wise.

'Oh yes. You see, once the sea was everything. The whole earth, everything was covered by the sea. But the earth has been fighting the sea all these years, ever since the beginning of time, pushing the sea back and back. So now, there isn't that much sea left. And you can see how crumpled the earth is. From pushing and pushing the sea.'

She said nothing for the sea still seemed very vast to her.

'So the sea cries and cries all the time so it can grow and cover the whole earth once again. And we are its tears, its children.'

She was both confused by this and frightened at the idea of the sea covering everything, even the barbecues on the mountain top. So she hurriedly moved the shell from her ear so that she wouldn't have to hear any more. She always did this when the shell spoke of things that felt threatening. Or else she changed the subject to inconsequential things. Such as the bad behaviour of all the little shells lined up on the barbecue and how to control them.

But more and more when she went into the house she missed the sea shell terribly, and one day when she was about to leave the barbecue she finally screwed up her courage and asked her if she could take her home.

'Oh no no no,' the shell cried in horror. 'I do not wish to be separated from the other shells. For then I would be as lonely as you are. With nobody to talk to and nobody to play with.'

She quickly moved the shell from her ear so she wouldn't have to hear any more. For although what the shell said was true, she thought it was a shameful thing and certainly didn't want anyone to know. The shell could be so cruel though for another time she said, '*My* mother is the sea, *my* father is the sky. Where are *your* mother and father?' That time she got so angry with the shell that she flung it into the sand and stomped off, vowing never to return again to talk to a creature so rude.

So she tried to stay away but it was very hard for what the shell said was true: she really was very lonely and had no one to play with. Except for the shells. So she went back and hung her head and picked up the shell and apologised.

'Please forgive me,' she said as her grandmother had taught her to say, 'I am most dreadfully sorry.'

After a pause the shell said, 'Oh that's alright. I am sorry too. It is excessively ill mannered to introduce into polite conversation subjects that are painful.'

But after that they found that they were still embarrassed and could find nothing to say to each other and the shell cleared her throat several times and each was thinking hard of something nice to say until the shell, wanting to make amends burst out with, 'You know what? *I* shall take you to the sea.'

'You?'

'Of course. I came here from the sea didn't I? So I can find my way back.'

And she said, 'Of course. What better person to go to sea with than a sea shell. You really would take me?' she breathed, not quite believing.

'Oh yes. I never fail to do anything that I promise to do,' the shell said huffily. 'We shall go on Sunday. Sunday is the best day for that is when the beach is full of children. There will be lots of people for you to play with. Come on Sunday morning very early and we will set out for the sea.'

The sea! She could hardly believe it. She was going to the sea.

I *shall* take you to the sea, she sang as she ran home.

I *will* take you to the sea.

I *can* take you to the sea.

When she got home she felt so excited that she had to tell someone. So that evening she whispered to Cherry who was helping to get her ready for bed:

'Cherry, guess what?'

'What?'

'Can you keep a secret?'

'Keep it to me 'eart. Don't laugh. Don't talk. Don't skylark,' Cherry laughed. 'What?'

'Tomorrow-I-am-going-to-the-sea,' she whispered.

'Liard!' said Cherry who was very direct and knew everything that went on in the house and knew that nobody was going to the sea tomorrow or any other day. 'Yu love mek-up story too much. Who tekking you to sea?'

'A friend,' she whispered, already crestfallen and sorry that she had shared her secret with Cherry for whenever she tried to share her secrets the same thing happened.

'A friend?' Cherry said scornfully. 'Which friend? You don't have no friend.'

She wanted to say, well you are my friend. Sometimes. Instead she tossed her head and stuck out her mouth and cut her eyes at Cherry and got into bed without speaking to her again. She would show her! But her heart began to beat so fast that she could hardly sleep and she tossed and turned all night in feverish dreams with a roaring in her ears as loud as an angry sea.

In the morning she woke up feeling wracked with pain and really ill and instead of getting better in the days that followed she got worse and worse until the doctor was sent for. And among other things she heard the doctor say that she needed plenty of bed rest and absolutely no excitement, it was bad for her heart, for she had had rheumatic fever. And so for weeks on end she stayed in bed, first in a haze of sleep and medicines. Then as she got better it was as if the entire household conspired to be nice to her, to coddle and entertain her.

Grandma moved her sewing machine into her room so she could talk to her as she sewed. Maud was in and out of the room all day with some new concoction from the kitchen and unbent enough to tell her Anansi stories. Grandpa taught her to play draughts and checkers in the time before supper. Even Marse George the penman who was very shy would sometimes come in the evenings and sit in the doorway of her bedroom, singing hymns softly. Best of all she had Cherry around her night and day, Cherry to teach her riddles and rhymes, fill her head with songs and nonsense verses of which she had an endless repertoire:

Wapsie kaisie cum pindar shell
Wapsie kaisie cum pindar shell.

The shell! She hadn't thought of the sea shells for a long long time, first because she had been too ill, then because she had been so engrossed in the life of the household with everyone trying to please, trying to make her well again. But now she started thinking of the shells again, for as she got back to normal so the household too seemed to resume its normal course in which nobody had much time for her. Grandma wheeled her sewing machine back into her own room saying now she was out of bed she did not need her any more. Maud ceased to bring her delicacies and had no more time for Anansi stories. Cherry had found or been given back all her household chores and had little time for what she now called foolishness and Grandpa found it less and less convenient to play draughts and Chinese checkers. It was as if time had speeded up for a while but was slowing back down again to a pace of such boredom and emptiness the days actually seemed to falter.

She became acutely conscious again of her loneliness. She began to spend more and more of her time thinking of the shells, yearning for the day when she would finally be well enough to be left to wander off on her own, to walk over to the barbecues where the shells would all be anxiously waiting to hear what had happened to her. And her friend would tell her all the news and they would plan another trip to the sea. She would enquire if the little shells had been behaving and whether the sea was rough or smooth today (for the sea shell said that all who came from the sea, no matter where they ended up, whether whole or in little fragments, continued to carry a part of the sea with them forever and ever). And she felt happy knowing that the shells were there, waiting.

Finally one day the doctor, Grandma, everyone, seemed to agree that she was completely well (but no excitement, mind, the doctor kept telling Grandma and she wondered each time exactly what he meant). So she headed for the barbecues and sang the seasong which popped into her head and as she neared them, she could almost hear the sea shells, tremulous, waiting to answer her in chorus:

I *shall* take you to the sea
I *will* take you to the sea
I *can* take you to the sea

But as she got within sight of the barbecues she saw in a blinding flash that the entire barbecue, all the barbecues were covered totally with pimento berries, a sea of them, and that nowhere in a corner of the top barbecue or anywhere else was there a truck load of gleaming sand or even the slightest hint that it had ever been there, until falling on her hands and knees and searching in the grass she found beneath the blades traces of sand and, finally, a glint of mother-of-pearl, a tiny fragment of a shell and nothing else. Bewildered, her heart beating so hard she could hardly breathe, she held it to her ear just as a great wave came tumbling over the mountains from the sea.

See the Tiki-Tiki Scatter

However long we were loved, it was not long enough.

Muriel Rukeyser

SHE floated aimlessly in rooms of dark corners and silences.

Outside, servants laughed loudly and the dogs barked ferociously at the cats.

But that was outside.

Inside, a film which had settled on the house long before she ever came there now sealed her off too, inside this special kingdom in which there was neither love nor hate or indeed much of anything. Night was marked off from day by the lighting of the lamps and evening prayers. That was the night-time ritual. Shadows from the breadfruit tree dangling over the tank would veer wildly in the huge room, now blue, now the exposed moss green plaster of several years back. Grandma would tuck her into the huge four-poster with the furry blanket lying ponderously on top and she would stretch out her hand and trace the mark of her black crayon on the vanity which was champagne coloured and cool and comforting to the touch.

> After the ball is over
> After the break of dawn

Grandma would sing, her thin voice wobbling like a wind-up gramophone unwinding,

> After the dancers leaving
> After the stars are gone

she would sing along with her. They knew only two songs – one and a half, really – or so it seemed for they did not know all the words of either one. Both, Grandma said, from the War. But what War? And had Grandma fought in it for her voice to be so broken? Or was it before the War? She was never sure. She liked the other song best for she could extract from it all the drama that was lacking in the first:

Oh brrr–EAK the NEWS to MO–ther
And TELL her that I LOVE her

she would sing passionately, dramatically, sometimes getting so loud that the bubble of film that covered the house would almost burst and Grandpa would cry from the living room: 'Hush'.

Every night it was the same. The two songs with Grandma and then prayers said kneeling on the cold floor and Grandma tucking her into bed and kissing her goodnight. Except for Sunday night. Then Grandma read to her from *The Sunday Book of Living Verse* which was all about dead and dying children, or so it seemed. 'It is the last New Year, Mother, that I shall ever see . . .', her favourite, every Sunday helped to send her to a watery sleep.

Daytime, the only rules covered meal times which were set and rigid. Then some mornings Miss Jones came and taught her Lessons. Miss Jones was scared of Grandpa and Grandma, of displeasing them, and so manufactured good news to report: her reading is excellent and her writing is improving and she seems to be understanding sums.

Then there were afternoons. There seemed to be a slowing down of the day as everyone rested, even Cyrene the cook having washed up and tidied away after lunch was resting in her room. And Grandma and Grandpa inside the house in their separate bedrooms snoring softly, much softer than their night-time snores. The world was in hush. And in good weather, which was almost always, she sneaked out of the house and headed for the pond.

The pond had been created in a natural hollow at the bottom of the garden. Grandpa over the years had built a wall to strengthen the sides and the top of the wall was smoothed over at the level of the ground and formed a flat walkway. At the shallow end as the wall got lower and lower it began to curve inwards on both sides, thus never meeting in a complete circle but forming a pathway into the pond itself. Occasionally, if there was no rain and the other ponds were dried down, the cows were allowed in and they waded in at the shallow end and made a mess. But usually the cows were not allowed into this pond. Nobody used this pond. It was just there. And it belonged to her.

Well, what other kingdom was there for her to claim? Inside the house was ruled over by Grandma and Cyrene; outside, Grandpa ruled everything – the endless pastures, the cattle, the citrus groves, the pimento walk, the woods in ruinate, the tenant farmers at the far end; sometimes slowly he would ride over his property, surveying all. God ruled the clouds and sky. She had thought to claim the area at the back of the house between the kitchen and the tank, over to where the maids' cottage was on one side and the cocoa walk on the other. But even Peggy the young maid who was normally so sweet tempered would chase her away from there. 'No. No white people back yaso,' she would yell at her. 'Go weh. Back to yu big house.' The backyard was clearly Peggy's territory.

The pond now and the poinciana tree hanging over it not even Grandpa seemed to want. So she became ruler and she had her subjects: millions of tiki-tiki and three pond turtles that Grandpa referred to as Columbus and his ladies. Columbus like his namesake, was a wanderer and explorer. Although this pond was his home, from time to time he would travel to others. Usually this happened when the pond had dried down to caked brown flakes of mud clinging to the sides and a slimy green mess at the bottom, when even the dragonflies deserted for a more welcoming bit of water. The time when Grandpa would have the men clean out the pond. At times like these Columbus and his two ladies would emerge on to the grass and proceed in sad and silent procession to Dimity's Pond which was two fields beyond. Dimity's Pond was fed by a spring and always filled with water. But even so, Columbus regarded the pond at the bottom of the garden as his real home for when the October rains began to fall and that pond filled again, he and his ladies would stumble on that painfully slow journey back across the pastures and she would anxiously follow their progress, their passing no more than a parting of the long grass, a shiver of the blades. Of course during the year Columbus and his ladies would make shorter day trips or else they would crawl up on to the concrete paving to sun themselves. But most of the time you would not even know that the turtles were there except for a sudden agitation in the water if one broke the surface for a moment. Then the tiki-tiki in their millions would scatter.

The tiki-tiki were her real subjects for they never entirely abandoned her.

Throw a crumb on top of the water and see how fast they come leaping from the depths; throw a stone in the water and watch them scatter. Most of the time though, if left undisturbed, they darted back and forth in the water, so many of them passing and repassing each other endlessly. Never colliding, never touching. Darting swifter than the swallows.

At first she had timidly watched them from the shallow end, for she couldn't swim and was afraid of water. She was scared of the deep end for the water there was dark from the ugly slimy green moss that lived there. The deep end was so deep you could hardly see anything for the sunlight did not penetrate and even the tiki-tiki you couldn't see very well unless you called them to the surface.

But little by little she was drawn to this end for the top of the wall was smoothed over and formed a perfect stage, about two feet wide, for her concert performances.

Every afternoon now as soon as the house fell silent and the thin snores rose from the grandparents' rooms, she would in a flash leap up from the bed where she had been put to rest and let herself silently out of the house. She would head for the pond, beginning to sing even as she approached. She knew only two songs, or one and a half, and never knew beforehand which one she would start with. If it were 'After the Ball' she would sing slowly and mournfully as she waltzed across the paved edge of the pond:

Many a heart gets bro-ken
If you could read them all
Many a da-da-di-da-DAH
AFTER THE BALL.

She usually ended on a strong note and a pirouette, pleased with herself. She might sing this song many times, over and over, going through the same paces, slowly moving and turning as if in rehearsal for something. Sometimes before she started the next song she might slowly peel an orange in order to have something to throw into the pond. Each time a bit fell in the tiki-tiki would scatter then swarm before disappearing in disappointment. Sometimes she never bothered to sing the words but la-di-daed her way, waltzing from one side of the pond to the other.

Her favourite though, was 'Oh break the news to Mother' for with this she could be as loud and expressive as she pleased and in the afternoon, Grandpa, nobody would hear her.

Oh burr-EAK the NEWS to MOTH-er
And TELL her that I LOVE-er

She enunciated slowly and carefully. And loudly to the skies.

And TELL her NOT to WAIT for MEEE
FOR I'M NOT COMING HOOOOOOOME.

The best part was coming up and she took a deep breath before attempting it.

Oh SAY there is no OTHER
Can take the Pull-ACE of Mo-THER.

She would look to Columbus and his ladies in the pond for approval after singing these lines and would end on a triumphant note, acknowledging the applause from her subjects – three pond turtles and a million tiki-tiki (passing dragonflies who hovered to listen of no-count for they were so transient).

She gave the song each time new interpretations, new flourishes. And this could go on for the entire afternoon.

La da da di la da da
For I'm not coming HOOOOM.

Sometimes she would finish in time to sneak back in before the household came awake, but more often than not she would be brought sharply back to reality by the sound of Peggy's voice nearby, calling her name. Then she would make her way back as fast as she could to the house and supper.

Every day the same things happened. Breakfast and then Miss Jones droning on and then lunch and then the afternoon visit to the pond. And after a time this became the part of the day worth living for and nothing could keep her away – the sudden freedom, the total control she exerted over this sphere, bewitched her. And the turtles and the tiki-tiki welcomed her afternoon visits, she could tell. What else was there to brighten their day? No, she had to be there now every afternoon. This was her duty. She could not disappoint them.

And more and more she became drawn to the dark green depths of the pond, the deep end. Sometimes instead of bursting into song the moment she arrived as her subjects expected her to do, she would lean over and peer deep into the depths beyond where the tiki-tiki hovered, trying to penetrate the water, deep deep down, to the end of the earth, even. More and more it became harder to tear herself away from the pond for in the water she met another face like hers that seemed to pull and pull her. The face *looked* like hers but could it be that of the dying boy in the *Sunday Book of Living Verse?* The soldier sending news to his mother? How did they find it there the other side of the world? Each time she felt herself pulled and pulled; only with great effort could she pull herself back, away from the pond, back into the world of the poinciana tree that was turned right way up again. She laughed then at the tiki-tiki as if showing her mastery, pirouetted and sang gaily

Oh SAY there is no OTHER
Can take the place of MOTHER.

But slowly, slowly, the game changed again. She no longer leaned over the pond to peer into the depths. Instead a reckless mood took hold of her. She would dance and spin closer and closer to the edge, spinning till she was breathless, falling around on the grass beyond the edge. Instead of putting her all into expression, into interpretation of the songs, she now rattled them off at quite a pace for she felt a speeding up of everything as if the world itself had gone out of control and was speeding too. More and more she laughed at the spectacle she must present to her subjects watching below. How entertained they must be by her speed dancing! As for the face in the water, the boy dying in the new year, the mortally wounded soldier, how surprised they would be if one day she actually spun right off into the water to join them the other side. How fascinated her subjects would be! Dignified Columbus and his ladies. What fun to go under. To see the dark green mosses parting. See the tiki-tiki scatter.

The View from the Terrace

from the dumb
precipice
an unknowing plant blooms
singing into the air

Rilke: Exposed on the Heart's Mountains

I

THE house suddenly appeared to him one morning after he had
spent two days in bed. Marcus wheeled him out to his accustomed place at the table on the terrace and the sight struck him
immediately. How could it not? It was an abomination, a
desecration, a heresy, a sight unbelievable. There was a house
on the hillside! *His* hill, the one which overlooked the village and
which his terrace faced. It was a small house to be sure; he
estimated it to be no more than twenty feet by twelve, with one
door and one window on the long side which faced him, no
more, from this distance, than a doll's house, or what a child
might draw; a wooden hut similar to those which sprung up
daily in the squatter settlements which everywhere littered the
hillsides ringing the city, visible evidence of a society out of
control. But his hillside wasn't a squatter settlement and no
other house marred his view. His house sat on a slight rise above
the village in the valley and from there he had an uninterrupted
view of the mountains on all sides. Far away there were houses,
proper ones, that is; but none close enough to mar his vision.

It had never occurred to him that the hillside he gazed at

every day would ever be defaced with human habitation, it was so steep and inhospitable. Few trees grew on it except for the occasional clump of mangoes; mostly it was covered with wynne grass which burned every year in the dry months and agaves which from time to time flowered yellow. Halfway up the hill and directly in front of his favourite seat on the terrace was the only tree of any size and this was a silk-cotton tree which would one day become a giant but which was still small as cotton trees go. Year after year he watched its progress as it shed its leaves in the winter months and turned a bright green in the spring. And now immediately behind this tree, as if sheltering in its arms, someone had built a house. On *his* hill. It wasn't really his hill but who else was there to claim it, who else had gazed at it three hundred and sixty five mornings every year for the past twelve years?

His first feelings of outrage quickly turned to scorn as he wondered which idiot would choose to put a house in such a godforsaken place. How ever would they get to it? The first dry season fire would devour it, the first rains would erase it. And then he wondered who could be so fearless as to build a house right at the root of a silk-cotton tree, or hadn't they heard, didn't they believe like all the other black people that duppies lived at cotton tree roots? But in these times anything was possible, even the old beliefs and superstitions which had lasted hundreds of years were being swept away, everyone now believed he was a god, tossed aside was all habit, all rules, all certainty. Even duppies and cotton trees weren't feared anymore. It must be one of those godless ganja-smoking Rastafarians who had put a house there, who had no respect for anybody or anything, who probably wanted a place to stash his weed, far from the law, for the village police would be far too lazy to walk up that hill and investigate and these days, with everything out of control, there was nobody in charge anyway.

And yet, as he examined the house more closely, which wasn't close since he didn't see all that well, he had to admit that it seemed neater and trimmer than any squatter's house he had ever seen, set squarely on blocks, the boards tight. Mr Barton admired neatness, things done well, and was inordinately proud of the ship shape condition of his own house; although not a carpenter, he had stood over the ones that built it and supervised the placing of every board, every nail. But then he was a careful man and had worshipped more than anything else the notion of a world that was well made, ordered, where everything followed an ordained path and everyone knew his place. And now this crazy little house, so out of place on the hillside. How on earth had they got the lumber up that slope, how had it gone up so quickly and even more important, who on earth planned to live there?

II

He didn't find an answer to this last question though having nothing else to do, he watched all day. But next morning there it was; as he went on to the terrace his eyes immediately lifted to the hill, to the house now planted securely in the centre of it mid-way between village and sky and there, framed in the doorway, stood a woman. It was too far away to make out her features but she appeared large, elemental, filling the doorway. She was moving her body and gesturing and then he noticed movement below her on the hillside and he saw the children, one, two, three, so tiny that they were visible only because of the bright colour of their school uniforms, bobbing up and down like balloons on strings as they raced down the hill disappearing behind the cotton tree and then reappearing in front as they followed a path that curved, now disappearing again behind a clump of bush, now reappearing, then finally disappearing in a stand of mangoes just behind the village. The woman stayed in the doorway a long time before she moved inside, but the door remained open. All during breakfast which Marcus always served him on the terrace he kept glancing up at the house, but there was no sign of activity till, suddenly, the woman appeared from behind the house carrying something in both hands and soon he realised what it was, a washtub, for she started to hang out clothes on the line and he knew right away that there was a baby in the house for even at this distance he could see that most of the laundry was undoubtedly nappies. Three children and a baby, the woman and – presumably – a man, in such a tiny house!

What manner of woman was this who in two days could move into a house built overnight, be able on the bright dawn to send her children off to school, their clothes newly pressed and shining clean he had no doubt, and, most marvellous of all, get whoever it was that had built her the house to build her a clothes line so quickly?

He remembered, jolted by the memory for he had not thought of her in a long time, how his first wife Maria had waited weeks for him to put up a clothes line after they had moved into their first new house, weeks uncomplaining while he fussed with his papers, his documents, his pictures, his 'study'. She had finally got someone else to do it. But then she had been of the finest breed of woman, silent, uncomplaining, understanding that the man she had married was on the way to the top and had more important needs to fulfill than any demands she could make. But that was precisely why he had married her. His wife he had chosen like the clothes he was now able to wear, like the house, the neighbourhood, his friends. She suited him. She was a light skinned girl from the country, several shades lighter than he, of a good family like his own: her father had been a druggist in town and also ran the small farm on which they lived and her mother a schoolteacher, and though they would have preferred her to marry the white soldier from Camp who was also courting her, she was an only child and much indulged and they gave in when they saw no prospect of moving her.

Henry knew that her mother found him too dark, though he was not as dark as her own husband, but they wanted Maria to marry up, to lighten the colour. But they also recognised him as a young man of high ambition and good prospects in the civil service which was just beginning to open up to talented young men of colour such as he, and his parents were as respectable as they were, indeed had far more land and money. Maria was young and pretty and would favour all her life shades of beige, grey and delicate pastel colours which belied the inner life she lived which was a state of constant anxiety to please him, though as time went on it became harder and harder to do so. But by that time the trying mattered only to her since he spent more and more time at the office and later, as he rose upwards in the ranks, served on important boards and commissions, at the club where he rubbed shoulders only with men like himself, frenzied men who were determined at all costs to make it, to prove beyond a doubt that they were just as capable as the white men who were pulling out, 'going home' after thirty or forty years in the colonies, but better than the black men who were jostling them, were, if truth be told, passing them – on the playing fields, in the professions, in wealth made in ways the brown man wouldn't stoop to for the white man hadn't.

But he was already firmly up the ladder, was one of those who would be left behind to run things when the white men finally left, who would manage the offices, the public works and the institutions, who were becoming doctors, lawyers and now, politicians. But the latter made Mr Barton too anxious and when the boys in the club began to talk politics as they did more and more nowadays, of freedom and decolonization and radical words like that, he would nod and smile but he would unobtrusively leave for he hated these words. He knew that they heralded the changes in the air and that, ironically, men like himself would be the beneficiaries of whatever the politicians managed to do. But he preferred to live a life that was as little disturbed as possible, that would enable him to strive upwards until he reached the level from which he could unobtrusively step not just into the post, the job of the white man who was leaving soon, but into the kind of life he lived with its easy nonchalance, the kinds of suits he wore, the kinds of jokes he told, the kind of food he ate, a style projected which Mr Barton was born to acquire. This style was all, for it enabled him to transcend everything that he hated about his own country, his own people, his parents themselves, a coarseness of behaviour, a loudness, an overamplification, an overfriendliness, a failure nowadays to observe the lines that in the past had been so strictly drawn and which he believed should continue to be, the certainties that regulated behaviour between the races, between bosses and employees, between men and women. His own behaviour was examplary in this respect for he strictly observed those rules which he had set himself, which he had spent a lifetime observing in those whom he considered his superiors; no one at any time could fault him for lack of 'correct' behaviour.

Nights when he left the office or club early enough he would find still awake and bent over their homework his children who gratified him greatly, his three light skinned straight haired children – no throwback there! – who would 'pass' in London or New York where he intended to send them, who were bright and anxious to please and did well in school, at piano and voice lessons, debating societies, sports and an endless round of activities. He generously attributed credit for whatever these children were to their mother, for raising them was her role. He played no part in the matter of their day-to-day upbringing unless it was to punish the boys which – rarely required – he did firmly and fairly with his strap on a Sunday which was the only day he was ever home. Most of that day – unless he had to go to the office – he spent with his family; he worshipped with them at the Parish Church where the governor and top civil servants, the best people worshipped – although he had been brought up a Methodist and his wife a Presbyterian. After church they would ride around for a while in the big black Austin he had just bought, drive where they could be seen, before going home to the heavy Sunday meal cooked by Myra who had been Maria's childhood nurse and who had been sent when she married to take charge of domestic responsibilities, and afterwards a short doze until the cool of the evening. Then they might visit or receive visitors and on Sunday evenings after supper, he would play games with the children or listen to them sing, or recite, or play the piano, while he gently dozed with his eyes wide open which was something he had also learnt to do from his former English boss, coming awake in time to loudly applaud them.

Occasionally he would take his family for a picnic in the hills and they often came to the village where he now lived, which was then the limit of the driveable road out of the city and where they would picnic on the bank of a stream. Often they would climb a hillock where many huge trees grew and leaning against a tree with his jacket off, his tie loosened, his family murmuring around him, he would fantasize about building a house just here, on this very spot ringed in by the mountains, facing the hill which was bare of everything but the wynne grass and agave but which in its very bareness, so unlike the rest of the over exuberant countryside where trees ran riot and wiss choked everything, achieved a kind of purity which was like a paradigm of what he would like his life to become – uncluttered, unviolated, full of certainties, shorn of anxieties.

Even as a small child in a large and noisy family he was sure that this was what he wanted from life, to be cut adrift from everything that was loud, that was offensive, that cut across too many boundaries and left one uncertain; to find a peace in things that were far away, alien even, like the mountains now. This peace which in time, unknowing, was achieved by nothing less than an alienation from the people around him – including his own family – first came to be crystallised in the poetry that Mrs King taught them in school and – when she discovered his 'sensitivity' and talent – encouraged him to write. Poems about daffodils and the downs and snow and damsels in distress, brave knights and languishing flowers and a world that somehow seemed rooted on its axis, steeped in values, in traditions that he failed to find or grasp in the real world that he inhabited. When he had won the scholarship to high school, his English teacher Mr Wimple who was himself English continued to nourish this side of his existence. After leaving school he was fortunate enough to acquire a succession of English bosses in his climb to the top who appreciated his 'sensitivity', his liking for things 'civilised', i.e. English. And this bare hillside facing this lush valley had come over the years to distill here at home a consciousness that was never far beneath the surface, of another, well-ordered life.

He began to fantasize about building a house facing the hill and at first it was nothing, but a fantasy for his salary was barely enough to keep them at the standard of respectability which they had reached. But he was a careful man and month after month eked out some savings. And then his father died and left him some property which he promptly sold and in time he was able to buy the land. He told nobody about any of these transactions, not even his wife, and for years it was his private joke that even as they picnicked and lay on the grassy knoll, his property, she knew nothing about it. And she died without knowing, for it wasn't until after she was gone that he had started to build there, at first as something to fill his empty Sundays. The house had remained a weekend retreat until he retired and moved into it.

He felt smug now when he thought of his own large, roomy shipshape dwelling and the foolish, crazily built shack on the hillside. Time and again he asked himself, 'Who is this ridiculous woman and why is she so foolish to accept any man's offer to build her a house in such an unproductive spot?' For he knew, even if she didn't, that nothing would grow around the house, nothing but the wynne grass that blanketed the shaly hillside. And he also knew that she would not be there long enough to grow anything. With the first May rain, he fully expected the house to slide down the hillside and out of his life as if it had never really existed.

III

But the house on the hillside stayed, months became years and the silk-cotton went through its endless cycle of change, getting larger with the years, shading more and more the little house behind it in spring when it put on mint-green leaves; exposing it to a harsher gaze when it shed them. Every weekday morning just after dawn the children started down the hill to school, pressed and shining. And their number grew. Now it was four children going to school, and still there were nappies on the line.

Astonishingly, he had never seen a man at the house though he looked several times a day, every day. All he ever saw was the woman, in the doorway or at the clothes line, and the string of children going off to school or coming up the hillside, playing in the evenings or at weekends in the small square of dirt around the house, but never a man. Where did these children come from, how were they fed and clothed, sent off to school every day? How a new child every year?

Mr Barton could easily have asked Marcus all these questions: who these people were, why they had chosen to live there, who the father was, was he crippled, sick, did he stay inside the house every day, did he live overseas, returning once a year? If Marcus did not know himself he could find out. But he had failed to ask Marcus from the very start for although he was not an imaginative man, there was a mystery here that intrigued him, a mystery that he wanted to keep close to himself and after a while, the house on the hillside, the woman braced in the doorway, the string of children, the absent father, became a secret obsession, a new and exciting dimension to his world which was more and more bound to this terrace, this house, this finite universe that his life had become.

Ever since Josie his second wife had left him or he had thrown her out, he was never sure which, he had lived there alone with Marcus who looked after him, faithful Marcus who had been in his household since boyhood. His children still phoned occasionally but had ceased visiting after he had let known repeatedly to each in turn the extent of his disappointment in them. All three had made a promising start. Raymond the eldest, a handsome boy, fine sportsman, bright, matriculated young. His father had encouraged his ambitions to be a lawyer and articled him to the finest firm of solicitors, but he had made his real break when the war came and he volunteered to join the RAF. He never got further than training camp in Montreal before the war ended, and he decided to stay on there and get his law degree at McGill. He married a Canadian girl, became more and more Canadian himself and much to his father's disappointment seemed to have lost all interest in the West

Indies thereafter, visiting infrequently and after the death of his mother not at all. He had never invited them to Canada or brought his wife and children to meet them. Before she died Mr Barton's wife made the only statement in their married life that had ever made him really angry, which was that Raymond did not want his wife and her family to know that the family he came from was not strictly 'white'. He had railed at her for her 'nonsense' but from time to time returned to the idea like gnawing at a sore tooth, to the nagging bitter feeling that she might very well have been right.

Mark too had done well, had got by on scholarships and was now a very senior lecturer at the university but he too had disappointed. In the opposite way to Raymond. His father cut him off totally after he had married in England and brought home a coal black girl – never mind that she was Doctor-Somebody herself; the bitterness of the quarrel between father and son was such that they had not spoken to each other for fourteen years.

And his daughter. He had come as close to his daughter as he had ever come to a human being, she had made up for the other disappointments of his life. Pretty, bright, dutiful. His gravest mistake was to have allowed her to go to the local university. He wasn't sure why she wanted that sort of education at all since she would soon find a nice husband to take care of her. He had encouraged her to go to Miss Simpson's and take a typing course which was what the nice girls were doing, but she was adamant about wanting to be a doctor. She had the same quietly stubborn streak as her mother, and when on her own initiative she took the university scholarship exam and passed, they had to give in. She had gone to live on campus as was required in those days but they had had her home every weekend, he secretly proud of her growing independence, her poise, her cheerful sweetness. And then, about her fourth year (had it happened slowly or crept up without their noticing?) she had started to change, to come home less and less, was even starting to argue with her father, to sass him, and then it had come out into the open, that she was getting more and more involved in radical politics and – it still pained him to think about it – finally became inextricably mixed up with Martin Howe, a disgrace to a well known family name. A notorious communist agitator who was on everybody's list from the local CID to Scotland Yard and, he had no doubt, Interpol. After the quarrels and after the break with her family she finally moved in, unwed, to live with him.

Though she eventually renounced Martin Howe and radical politics, became a well-known paediatrician, married a fine doctor and had three children, her father could never forgive her the agitation, the hurt she had caused him, blamed her for her mother's weakened heart. Whenever he thought of his family, and this was very infrequently nowadays, he wondered where their mother had gone wrong in rearing these children. Had she been too weak, too indulgent? For matters of child rearing clearly had been hers from the start.

When his thoughts turned to his own family he more and more wondered about the woman on the hill and her children, how she was raising them, whether she had ambitions for them as he had had for his; did she aspire to turn them into lawyers, doctors, teachers? How could she, she who had nothing but a crazy doll's house on a hillside, who lived alone, who created babies year after year, by magic, it seemed? For now there were five little children bobbing off to school and nappies still filled the line.

He loved the weekends best for the children were at home and there was such a buzz of activity around the little house. Now the cotton tree had grown some more and he was unable to see as clearly as he used to, but as the years passed new things were forever happening. At some point they acquired another little house half hidden behind the bushes, whether an outhouse or a kitchen he never knew. And miracle of miracles, around the house itself appeared one spring time colourful objects which stayed and stayed and which he was forced to admit were flowers. Then another time, overnight it seemed, the house acquired a coat of thin paint, yellowish, which somehow made it just right against the grass which was either purplish or yellowing and blackened, and the cotton tree which was either mint green or bereft of leaves. And the children seemed to him so happy!

They frolicked in the space around the house and had acquired a dog which frisked around them as they ran down the hillside in bright colours, red, yellow, blue, like balloons on strings bobbing up and down as they disappeared and reappeared at the same points in the path as they always did. Later, the dog's barking would come faintly first and then the children would follow with bright objects in their hands which he eventually came to recognise as plastic water bottles. And then he was able to distinguish one child from the rest, the eldest, a boy in a khaki uniform who went off to school every morning now before the others, making his way gravely alone down the path from the hill. On Saturdays they all played around the house, and faintly on the wind, he heard or thought he heard the sound of children's voices and laughter and the dog's excited barking. He didn't know why but the sound made him sad.

And always he wondered about the woman whom he never once saw stride down the path, though she must have, for some days when he looked up the door was closed, firmly locked against him. When he did see her she was either at the doorway or shaking something through the window or hanging out clothes on the line or taking them in; day after day, year after year there were always nappies on the line. Who was fathering these children, did he come so late at night, leave so early in the morning that he was never seen? No matter who the man was, it was the woman who held it all together, who bore these children, cared for them, sent them off to school pressed and shining. Sometimes he saw her as a mythical being standing in her doorway, ageless, timeless, like Sorolla's paintings of Valencian fisherwomen, large, elemental, muscled, braced against the sea, masculine in their strength, yet beautiful and dignified too; he had seen them in a museum in Madrid when he and Maria had visited Europe for the first time. He had wondered idly then what it would be like to make love to women like these, to be crushed in their strong arms, their muscled thighs, to be held breathless against their limitless bosoms, and now he wondered if it could have been like that with the woman on the hill. But then he had never had a real black woman, of all the young men he knew, because he had always found the idea a threatening force to his personal universe, something wild and untameable that could not be contained within the borders of his picture books.

IV

The visit to Europe had been the highlight of his life up to then, the 'home leave' that all top civil servants, those who had made it, dreamed of and planned for years. But although he would not have admitted it to anyone, it saddened him to realise that going to England did not, as he had imagined it would, feel like going home. He was for once acutely aware of his colour, his hair, his 'colonial' accent, of things which were a source of pride to him at home but which here seemed flat, provincial, out of place. The dismal climate, the greyness and dirt of London, the indifference, the icy politeness, were shattering experiences though he hid it well in his forced gaiety at seeing the Changing of the Guard, visiting the theatre, the cinemas, getting used to the Underground. He and his wife preferred the Mediterranean countries, Italy and Spain, where they looked as if they belonged; if it weren't for the language no one would have called them strangers.

Still, these people were *foreigners*! They bought hand-blown glass in Venice, Delft-ware in Holland, a painting of a bullfight in Spain and endless souvenirs. Looking back, he realised that all of them who had gone to Europe on 'home leave', year after year, ended up as if programmed at the same places seeing the same things, bringing home the same memories, the same souvenirs, treading a well beaten path as if each was afraid of branching out and somehow doing the wrong thing. And now these memories had passed through his mind like water – except the Valencian fisherwomen – and the souvenirs had long disappeared, probably during the time when his life had for a brief period lost its momentum, when things had gone slightly askew and he had allowed his house to be 'redecorated'. It was during the period when he was married to Josie – he still could not think of her without feeling his heart palpitating and something in his brain tightening with anger.

He had met her some time after Maria died. He had had no thought of ever marrying again. To him marriage was something undertaken once to fulfill an obligation to his parents, to society, it was something ordained if one aspired to a station in life, if one did not want to be considered odd or eccentric. There was nothing special or magical about it. Marriage, wife, children were so much a part of the civilised life to which he subscribed that they were taken for granted. He had certain obligations on his part and she on hers and as long as these were met, then the whole thing hardly bore thinking about. By the time Maria died, they had drifted so far apart, the exchange of mutual obligations had become so ingrained, so ritualised, that he hardly missed her. For those parts of his life which had intersected with hers continued as before. Myra prepared his meals as she had always done, looked after his clothes, the house, the shopping, and her son Marcus was now big enough to help in the running of the household. Marcus increasingly became the man-a-yard, the gardener, the butler, the chauffeur. Although he had paid for Marcus to go to school and learn a trade, Marcus had shown more aptitude for setting the table, cooking, driving and gardening than anything else and Mr Barton had done nothing to discourage him. He considered Marcus a born servitor, loyal, faithful, discreet and best of all, silent, and he rewarded his faithfulness well. When Myra had got too old and gone back to her 'country', Marcus had continued to occupy the cottage at the back of the house which was screened from its view by a thick shoe-black hedge. He had taken over so smoothly from her it seemed as if he had been doing it all his life, having no existence of his own outside of answering his master's calls at all hours of the day or night, a bell having been installed to connect the main house with the cottage after Mr Barton had suffered his first stroke. It gave Mr Barton a great deal of satisfaction to feel that he and Marcus, two men alone, could manage so well on their own without the company or assistance of women, except when Marcus went back to his 'country'.

Once a month Marcus continued a faithful habit begun in childhood, which was to visit the place where his mother came from and where they still seemed to have an enormous number of cousins, aunts, uncles and other kin and for whom, rain or shine, Marcus would take boxes and boxes of 'city' goods. He would take the bus on a Friday afternoon and return late Sunday, bringing for Mr Barton the 'country' food – yams, cocos, plantains and fruit – which were about the only native things that Mr Barton enjoyed, garrulous with the news of 'home'. This was really the only time that Marcus talked, and over the years Mr Barton had got used to this Sunday evening chatter though he hardly listened to anything that was said, as he never did to anyone except his superiors at work. But Mr Barton was glad that Marcus had this other life in the hills of Clarendon which seemed to be the only life he had outside of looking after Mr Barton. This Marcus did with scrupulous and tender care. He supervised Miss Mary from the village who came to wash and clean but he himself did the cooking and serving, mixed Mr Barton's evening drinks, fussed over his health and saw to it that he took his medicines and kept his doctor's appointments. He also cared for Mr Barton's old Mercedes Benz with the same love and diligence and when he could persuade him, took him for slow rides. Once a week on a Thursday afternoon he drove into town and brought up Mr Davies, Mr Fisher and Mr Solomon for their weekly bridge game with Mr Barton. They were retired like himself, two senior civil servants and a lawyer, and the weekly bridge game was the remaining diversion of their lives. Marcus would fix them drinks, serve them supper and at the end of the evening tenderly tuck them into the car and drive them home again.

Mr Barton regarded Marcus as his touchstone, as his treasure, though he never showed this in any way. He wondered if Marcus ever went into the village at night when he was sleeping, if he had friends there, if he had a woman or, he even speculated, a man, for Marcus sometimes seemed more womanly than man and anything was possible these days. But whatever Marcus did, his behaviour was impeccable, for not once did Mr Barton get a hint of anything happening in Marcus's life external to the household. In any event, he never speculated on Marcus's affairs for long for he had very little interest in other people's lives. All he knew was that Marcus was on call day and night, except for two nights each month when he went to his village in Clarendon and Mr Barton had to make do with Miss Mary.

V

Mr Barton always felt gratified when he thought of Marcus's life of service to him for surely it indicated that he could not be such a bad man after all. If he could inspire such loyalty and friendship from a servant, surely he could not be the 'self-righteous dinosaur' his daughter felt him to be, could not be the 'cold fish', the 'arrogant bastard', the 'selfish egomaniac' that Josie had accused him of being. But then, as he learnt to his great cost, too late, Josie was incredibly vulgar, the kind of woman who no longer knew her place, like the facety little black girls nowadays in the banks, the supermarkets, the doctor's office. They were everywhere, taking offence at the slightest attempt to correct their manners or their pronunciation, to let them know their place. Josie was just like them. Except that Josie was white.

In fact Josie had the whitest skin that he had ever seen on a human being, skin that was almost translucent, the blue veins showing, her complexion all pink and white, the perfect 'English rose', her arms, her legs, her body plump and dewy, almost pulsating. He had met her when he had accompanied the Chief to England for the banana negotiations and she had been one of the secretaries assigned to their delegation. He had been taken by her gleaming whiteness, her brisk cheerfulness that made her unlike any other woman he had ever met, astonishing him by talking to them with the utmost friendliness, to the Chief with a playfulness that pleased him. All the men on the delegation, six of them from the various West Indies territories all admired her greatly, he could tell, and he was astonished when on the third day she asked him home to dinner. He had accepted, assuming that by 'home' she meant a place where she lived with her mother and father for she was still very young, but home turned into a dreary climb into a grubby Victorian building to what was called a bed-sitter, something quite new to him since he had always stayed in hotels. One room furnished with a sink and a gas ring and a bathroom 'down the hall'.

Despite her efforts to make it cheerful, he was appalled that such a rose should inhabit such confined quarters and he was made particularly uncomfortable by the presence of the large bed which occupied most of the room. But she made him relaxed from the start because she herself was so relaxed, so natural, the most natural person he had ever met and because she poured the gin non-stop and she prattled on and on, mainly about the romantic tropics and how wonderful it must be to live in the sun all year. She questioned him about his life, his children, his car, his house, his view from the terrace in a way he would have found offensive coming from anyone else, but he was too entranced from the start, too flattered at this interest from a comely English rose to question it. She was a lousy cook and the dinner was burnt, but by then he had had so much to drink that he was almost unsurprised when they ended up in the bed. At least a part of him was unsurprised, the other self looked on as in a dream. Her behaviour in bed astonished him, almost frightened him because he had never once been unfaithful to his wife, indeed had never slept with anyone else, and his years of marriage had never prepared him for the fact that a woman could actually respond, actually enjoy lovemaking, much less take the initiative as Josie did. He was frightened, exhilarated, instantly, madly in love and by the time he left England ten days later, had proposed and been accepted.

But life with Josie had been hell from the start, five years of anxiety and suffering. Josie liked him well enough, was gay and loving, but she also liked a lot of other people; a round of parties, of 'mixing', and his life became a torment of watchfulness, of acrimonious quarrels, of a feeling of being out of control. She was in fact the first human being within his jurisdiction that he could not control. His first wife, his children while under his roof, had obeyed him implicitly, so did his employees. Even the friends whom he chose or who chose him, fell sway to his domineering personality which was softened by the fact that he was a generous host and a witty, if slightly mean, raconteur.

In short, few in his life had ever gone against him. But Josie did, for she acted exactly as she pleased, laughed at his strictures against her behaviour, her friends, his lectures on 'respectability'. She was the first woman in his existence who had a life of her own, who did things simply because they pleased her, who argued, who asserted herself. There was only one role he was equipped to play which was to resist, to the bitter end, this encroachment as he saw it on his authority, his manhood. And bitter it became. By the time he had got rid of her – for so he saw it – with a very substantial settlement, he felt that he had been through hell and back and was done with women forever. Following on the troubles with his daughter, the episode represented another time in his life that he had failed to determine the course of events. But how could he have, when women themselves had suddenly gone insane, were rejecting the direction, the protection, that their menfolk offered them, were recklessly plunging off on their own into unknown and unspeakable depths?

Increasingly, he felt empathy with the woman on the hill. She, at least, was doing what was natural to women, was being 'womanly', though how she managed he still could not imagine. But she was caring for her children, seeing that they went to school every day and she certainly had no time for running around. The cotton tree was growing bigger, the little house seeming to shrink behind it, and the string of children getting longer and longer.

VI

More and more he felt his age, felt that the time was coming soon when he would no longer be on earth, and he knew as the only certainty now, that the cotton tree, the house, this indomitable woman and her children would still be there, for all time, and that people like himself who had followed conventional paths, who believed in an ordained destiny were a breed passing away. It was the people with nothing but their lives, their vitality, like this woman on the hillside, like the other squatters all over the land, who were growing with incandescent energy, fuelled by the wind, by the air, by the boundless heritage of the universe. And he wondered where someone like Marcus fitted into these two worlds. He had left Marcus a substantial legacy in his will, enough to set him up modestly for life, and he speculated on what Marcus would do after he was gone, if it would be too late for him to create a new life of his own, freed from the demands and the restrictions of life with the Bartons. And how would be bridge the life that he now led, a life lived through another, with the life of the people like those on the hillside or of the 'country' where his mother came from?

For the first time in his life Mr Barton felt regret for the years he had spent with Marcus and failed to know him, accepting as only his due what Marcus gave him, failing irrevocably to enter into his life, to penetrate beyond his presence. More and more nowadays such thoughts came to him about Marcus, about Maria and his children, about his whole life, as if a door he never knew existed was opening wider and wider and he knew in some oblique way that such thoughts were bound up with the life of the woman on the hill. She had entered his consciousness and forced him to cross into unknown territory, to wonder, to speculate and to dream, despite himself. He was sensing an opening onto choices, the possibilities which all his life he had resisted. He began more keenly to feel, to admit his own loneliness, the separation of his life from others, his failure to bridge the gaps. And he also knew with profound sorrow that knowledge had come too late. It was this thought that made him angry, that made him begin to look again at the house on the hillside the way he had done when it first appeared, as an alien transient intrusion which would vanish in the first heavy rains of May.

VII

The rains that year did come in unspeakable torrents, the heaviest rains he had ever experienced in his long life; it rained for almost two weeks, without letup, so heavily that for the first time he was unable to stay on the terrace, to open the windows on that side and see beyond the whiteness outside, hear beyond the roaring of the river, the pounding in his head. He knew that the little house on the hillside was still there, for in those moments when the rain let up briefly, he went out onto the terrace to look and was astonished each time to see that it still stood in the shelter of the cotton tree. He felt guilty that he was here in his huge house, snug and shipshape, able to withstand rains like these without a leak, and that the mother and her family were there huddled together in this hut on a lonely hillside as the May rains came unceasing. Then there was a night when he thought his own roof would go, so heavy was the pounding from the rain, the heaviest they said afterwards in seventy years. And though he took his medicines and his sleeping pill, he slept restlessly for his waking and his dreaming alike were filled endlessly with the image of the woman on the hill and her children. He knew that by no miracle now could the little house stand.

When the rains cleared, he saw that the house on the hillside had really gone. Bits and pieces of zinc and wood scattered and shored up against the cotton tree were all that remained. And the woman? And the children? Something that might have been a sob broke from him. But he composed himself and buzzed for Marcus to ask him – finally – about the house on the hillside.

'Oh, Miss Vie,' said Marcus. 'We went and bring her and the children down from Monday night you know, sar, two of them is here with me right now and the rest of them with their mother over at Miss Iris yard.' In his joy at hearing that the woman and her family were safe he was also hearing as in parallel lines what Marcus was saying, faintly at first and then so loudly that it took over everything like the drumming in his head.

'So you knew this woman?'

'Oh yes, sar.'

'I mean you knew her all the time, since that house went up on the hill?'

'Yes, sar. I did help move her up there. Is my country she come from, you know. Remember I did tell you all bout it when she move here. Seven, eight year now.'

Mr Barton felt let down, as if he had been caught sinning. For all along he had speculated about the woman as a nameless, faceless stranger and he imagined that if she saw him at all from her doorway, she regarded him as the same. But now here was Marcus saying that he knew her, Marcus who went nowhere, who knew nobody. Marcus had helped this woman build her house, that desecration in front of his, Marcus who undoubtedly told her his name and probably everything about him, Marcus who since Monday night had been harbouring her children under his roof, Marcus who could have saved him endless anxiety since then, Marcus who obviously knew everything.

'So who is the father of all these children?' he demanded angrily. 'How come he is never seen?'

'Well is not one father you know, sar. The first one is for Supe, you remember Superintendent Atkins who used to be at the station here one time, that is how she come to come here, he in MoBay now but him mind him well. Jason, a bright little boy. And then Stephanie and Rosie is for Mr Binns that did manage public works here. Vinnie is for the soldier-bwoy, Miss Iris son Jake. And two of them is mine. Geffrard and Speedwell. Is my country she come from you know, sar.'

Mr Barton was staring at Marcus blankly as if he couldn't give credence to what he was hearing, so angry was he becoming. The woman was no better than the rest of them! A common whore! So many men! Marcus! Where did they meet? Did he go there? Did she come here! Did Marcus leave him alone at nights to meet her? Two of the children! Such absurd names! It was unthinkable! And he had known nothing. Nothing. How monstrous to live with someone for so many years and not know them, not know them at all!

Marcus was innocently looking at Mr Barton as he told him about the lady from his country and her baby-fathers all fine decent men who minded her, except for the soldier-bwoy Jake but his mother Miss Iris did her best. And the rescue he Marcus had organised with virtually the whole village taking part, which included some funny moments such as when a chamber pot got loose from a bundle and went rolling down the hill and only came to rest when it jumped on to the head of Mr Parkins the carpenter, who was coming up the path below fortunately he had on his felt hat but still and all. . . . Mr Parkins was a deacon in the church and had his dignity to protect and he was so mad for he didn't know at first what hit him and when he found out he was madder than ever for they were all laughing at him, even Miss Vie whose house about to mash flat in the rain. Marcus was laughing himself silly as he told the story – for in his own world he was considered as good a raconteur as Mr Barton was in his. And he thought that Mr Barton was enjoying the whole thing hugely, he looked so interested, as interested as he looked on Sunday evenings when he Marcus came back from the country. Poor old man, sometimes he made up all sorts of things to amuse him, thinking them up on the bus coming home; he had nobody else to tell him anything. And Marcus was enjoying telling Miss Vie's story so much that he wouldn't even have known when something burst in Mr Barton's head like rain.

A few days later, the house was back on the hillside. But now there was no one on the terrace to see it.

Lily, Lily

I

. . . the three little girls going to church? Elma, Sadie and Lily. Elma and Sadie are the daughters of Mr and Mrs Enos Montrose, better known — by the children — as 'Teacher and Teacher-Wife'. So Elma and Sadie are above reproach, children of the first family so to speak and they are always dressed simply (teachers' salaries being what they are) but impeccably, with manners to match (and you can't fault these refined, educated black people, you know) saying *Good Morning: Good Evening* left and right to everyone. And Lily? Oh Lily's background is even finer than that of the teachers' children for how else would she get to walk with them to church every Sunday? Lily is the daughter of Mr and Mrs DaSilva, solid, respectable people. O yes. Mr DaSilva owns the sawmill over at Rock Road and makes a good living from it too, especially now that money is flowing in from Cuba and Colón where all the men have gone and Mrs DaSilva is the unofficial godmother to one and all.

Mrs DaSilva is the head of Mothers Union and is the one who collects baby clothes for fallen women and gives them the appropriate lectures before handing the clothes over; who takes in the young 'schoolgirls' and teaches them to set table and serve at meals, to make beds properly and to dust, to make jams, jellies and cakes until they get too 'big and force-ripe' (as they say); some, despite her best efforts, even *enceinte* (ungrateful wretches!) so she has to get rid of them, post them back to their mothers, poor things, and get another schoolgirl to be broken in. But don't get me wrong, some of the schoolgirls have stayed with Mrs DaSilva until they are grown women and she has set them up in good jobs, even in Kingston, and found decent young men to marry the better ones and some, like our Lurline for instance, she has encouraged to start little money making projects on the side in jams and jellies, pickles and pimento dram, tatting, strawwork and embroidery. When we go to the Church Sale you will see that much of the work on display comes from Mrs DaSilva's girls (as she likes to call them). And then through the Mothers Union or the Dorcas Society or whatever, Mrs DaSilva organises visits to the sick and the old. She also holds classes for the more respectable girls of the town to teach them the finer arts of homemaking, including how to manage servants. So you see, she is busy all the time.

It is perhaps accurate to say that Mrs DaSilva is in charge of the domestic manners and morals of our little town here, and some of us were glad to hand that role over to her for even though my own dear mother was unquestionably the queen bee when she was alive, no one could hold a candle to her, (and in those days of course no brown woman would have dared try but we must accept changing times) and I will admit that poor Mama had expected me, Emmeline Greenfield, to carry on and uphold the family name as the arbiter of taste and values in the town but it is a fact that some of us are born intellectuals with no talent whatsoever for domestic activities, especially if we were encouraged to cultivate our minds by our Paters and we can't help but follow our stars even if it means we become a teeny bit radical and somewhat agnostic (though I will confess that the hardness of the bench in our pew did help me to become an unbeliever even faster than Papa's lectures), and we leave aside marrying because you know the men of today don't want women who operate at a high intellectual plane. They are far more interested in the fluffy, silly ones and some people simply will not compromise for the sake of a diamond ring, but as I was saying Mrs DaSilva is the most prominent lady in our town, though nowadays with all this travelling back and forth that's taking place (even Gladstone my gardener of twenty-five years took off with the rest of them to Colón last year), there is a whole new breed of people who have much money and little else, certainly no respect for manners or graces. One of these women from right here in our town, who not so long ago was walking the streets barefoot, looking for work as an ordinary domestic (I saw it with my own eyes), got it into her head to take off for Colón as a higgler if you please (thyme and skellion are her specialties, I hear) and you are not going to believe it, but a year later this same woman is back here wearing silks and satins (in broad daylight) *dripping*, just dripping with Panama gold from head to foot and this creature was actually rude to Mrs DaSilva only last week in Agostino's shop. She objected to Mrs DaSilva being served ahead of her because she said she was there first. And to show you how times are changing around here once upon a time Agostino would have put the impudent thing in her place, thrown her out of his shop once and for all and apologised handsomely to Mrs DaSilva but the cowardly man being more respectful of money than anything else, (like people of his kind, I can remember when his father first came here as a pedlar with a pack on his back, I was only a child then but at least he was properly respectful) this Agostino actually asked Mrs DaSilva to wait since that creature was there before her and he told Mr Foster afterwards that nowadays one cannot afford to offend these Colón people for they are the ones with the money, can buy and sell anyone in the town, including the DaSilvas. And poor Mrs DaSilva was so mortified, especially when some of those black people in the shop giggled as she swept out, and good thing her husband can afford it for she has vowed never to shop in this town again and who can blame her?

But where were we? What qualifies Mrs DaSilva for the role of leading lady, you were asking (bearing in mind that some of us are far too high minded and serious to claim it)? Well, she spent considerable time in Kingston before marrying Mr DaSilva and there – in what capacity we do not know – acquired the graces she now imparts freely and generously to all. Everyone (except those who don't know any better) agrees that Mrs DaSilva is a lovely lady, an asset to our town. And so without a doubt is her daughter Lily.

. . . but even as the beautiful and demure Lily walks down the street with the Montrose girls dressed in her best for church, dressed far more expensively than the teachers' children, even as Lily (whose manners are even more impeccable than theirs considering who her mother is) greets one and all, even as Lily's pure soprano rises from the choir loft every Sunday though she is only eleven, younger by far than anyone else in the choir but a voice like that! (Mrs Montrose who is the organist and choir mistress and arbiter of musical and other cultural tastes, or fancies herself to be, Mrs Montrose has great plans for Lily and her voice.) Even as after church Lily demurely greets one and all and walks sedately to the buggy with her mother and father, even as Lily smiles (and smiles), is there a hint, a smudge, an edge of uncertainty hovering over her?

We hasten to say it has nothing to do with anything that Lily has done for Lily is pure as her name, above reproach, a kind, loving, dutiful daughter, an exceptionally bright student (brighter than the teachers' daughters even, much to their chagrin) and a voracious reader (I know because I lend her books all the time); exceptionally talented (you will agree when you hear her voice) and you have seen for yourself that she is remarkably pretty.

If that Lily were not so pretty perhaps people would not notice her, would not gossip at all, but people are always commenting on Lily's extraordinary looks and one thing leads to another and next thing they look again and begin to wonder and, if they are really fas' (as they say), to whisper among themselves. For although Mr and Mrs DaSilva are both good looking (of that there is no doubt) people cannot figure out how they could have produced such a child as Lily. Lily, it is true, has Mrs DaSilva's eyes and forehead, a high intelligent forehead and exceptionally deep set yet large and limpid eyes in a long face, a bit like Clarissa Collins the socialite suffragette, (though of course *they* have never heard of her but her picture is right here in the *Illustrated London News* that's just arrived. It takes forever to get here but I can't do without it, a bad habit my dear Papa broke me into, getting all the London magazines and papers. One must keep oneself informed, you know, even if the people around here are so provincial caring for nothing but jams and jellies and rescuing fallen women and church socials). But as I was saying, Lily does have this long and striking face just like her mother's, in fact it's a family trait, known by all who know them as the 'Neal look' – they all looked alike, her mother, long dead, her older sister who was postmistress at Burnt Ground for forty years (this is Mrs DaSilva we are talking about now), and her niece Lily after whom her daughter was named and who is now the postmistress there. All have the same long face, the same high forehead, the deepest darkest eyes and the same thick and heavy head of hair, very striking women (as some of these respectable brown women really are). There is no question that Lily is a Neal but she has her father's mouth, which in his face is so incongruous for the rest of his features are rather coarse, you will see when you meet him (for we mix with *everyone* here, my dear), but he has this small bow-shaped mouth which looks funny on him but which is so very fashionable among women at this time and which on Lily looks fabulous.

All in all Lily has inherited the best features of both parents but one thing people cannot understand is how Mr and Mrs DaSilva are so dark (they really are, when you think of it though money whitens is the motto today) and Lily has come out almost white (white, you would say if you didn't know any better). Mr DaSilva especially is almost black, a dark brown man though his features are not really so bad all things considered, with wavy hair (when he plasters it down with Macassar Oil it doesn't look all that coarse) and the hair certainly is a throwback to some Portuguese ancestors somewhere. You can be sure if his hair didn't have this hint of straightness Mrs DaSilva would not have considered marrying him, respectable and well established though he is, (as she herself told someone) although, as you will see, Mrs DaSilva herself is quite dark – that lovely chocolate brown skin which unlike other white people I truly admire, the fine features and the thick curly hair that denote a throwback much closer than Mr DaSilva's to white or even Indian ancestors. Her grandmother she tells anyone who cares to listen (which is everyone) was a full white lady from Yorkshire, England (though she never said how she beached up at Burnt Ground) and on her father's side, *his* father was a white man from Ireland, etc. etc. etc. (though who would want to be related to the *Irish*?).

But when all is said and done white ancestors and all (though some of us have nothing *but* white ancestors and not one of them Irish), the fact remains that the skin of Mr and Mrs DaSilva is very dark and the skin of their child is very white and her hair is straight like a white person's and how does anyone explain that? Though to my mind people are just being fas' (as they say) for in truth a lot of people in this town could tell stories about throwbacks in their own families – worse yet when what gets thrown up is the black ancestor for *naturum expellas furca* . . . but I forgot you went to sleep in Latin classes. I mean, look at the McGregor twins with both parents acting as if they are white (though some of us know better), and one child comes out with whitish skin and very coarse red hair and one is dark with straight hair like an Indian. Then there is the case of the Lawrence family where the parents are identical brown people, same skin colour, same hair colour and texture, same eyes, everything, almost like twins themselves, and they have eleven children and every child it seems is a different shade so to speak, every type of racial combination though each is a Lawrence *sans doute*. There's a family look you know and the point I am trying to make is that these are all highly respectable families like the DaSilvas. For nowadays colour is no bar to respectability, not like it was in my mother's time, and besides, there is only one real white person left around here so I have to be broad-minded about these things or else who would I have to talk to (since friends like you visit so seldom). So given that in our little town we have so many examples of what race mixing can throw up

– or *down* (ha, ha, forgive my little witticism) why do people single out Lily so?

Ever since the child was born people have been talking, though what they have to talk about only God knows. Mrs DaSilva was properly attended to by Sister Dawn, then the midwife, (and properly trained at Victoria Jubilee Hospital School of Nursing too) who had delivered hundreds of babies – everyone born in town before Dr Shand came to settle – and if there are any secrets to be told (and what secrets could there be?) Sister Dawn has gone with them to her grave. And people who are really bad minded point out that Sister Dawn was Mrs DaSilva's aunt. She had been the one to introduce Mrs DaSilva to her husband in the first place when she came from Kingston to spend time with her – under rather mysterious circumstances too – and Sister Dawn would die to protect her family.

But really, I don't know how I have got myself mixed up in this business talking the same as the black people. (But you don't know how delicious it is to have someone of one's own set to talk to for a change, so forgive my little naughtiness.) Here I am talking as if there were some secret, some mystery about the most prosperous family of our town. People say that Lily is looking peaky these days but that is probably because she is studying so hard. She wants to get into St Catherine's of all places my dear, where of course only white girls used to go (or so it was in our time) but *plus ça change*. They are getting liberal these days and letting in a few respectable light-skinned girls, one or two at a time, because there are no longer as many white girls as there used to be to support these schools. (You remember a lot of the white families started fleeing from '65 when we were in school and many of them never returned.) I don't see a thing wrong with Lily going there. These institutions must change with the times and I have even written to the present Headmistress on her behalf (I treat Lily as if she were my own child she is such a dear little thing) and Lily has to sit an entrance examination, and to get in she has to do better than all of the white girls put together. I must say I really don't see anything wrong with that because it is all well and good to lower barriers, but they have to be lowered ever so gradually so that only the very best of the brown people are allowed in one at a time because if that were not done, the next thing is all the black people are crashing the gate, and how would you feel to know that the daughter of Miss-Higgler-to-Colón was getting into your old school?

But Lily, Lily is fine. She is almost white anyway and has had a most excellent upbringing (I have to give her mother credit for that though I have helped here and there to smooth off some of the rough edges, you know, but subtly so these people won't take offence). And it is true that Lily is looking peaky and has dark circles under her eyes. She looks even more than ever like her aunt or rather cousin Lily, the one she was named after, the way she looked that time when she came here ill and sad just a few months before Lily (our Lily) was born (six months to be exact). It was funny because Janie who was alive then and working with the DaSilvas found herself nursing two sick ladies for Mrs DaSilva suddenly discovered (after all these years of marriage and, presumably, trying ha ha) that she was expecting – three months gone! – and that her stomach upset was not 'nerves' as the doctor in Kingston had told her.

And Lily (the other Lily), O Lord! She was like a soul in torment, she stayed in the house all day and cried and hardly ate anything and wasted down to nothing (Janie said) and lived on soursop and condensed milk with a hint of nutmeg, the only thing she could keep down (strange!) and wasted away while Mrs DaSilva (we might call her Lucy at this stage since we know her so well), Lucy was getting larger and larger and more glowing, or so she was described to us by Sister Dawn and Janie and Mr DaSilva. For in those days ladies in a delicate condition really were confined to their homes if not to their beds – not like today where the young girls with their big stomachs are knocking you off the pavement brazenly without the slightest hint of shame – Mrs DaSilva especially being slightly old to be having her first child. (She is older than me I assure you though she doesn't look it, but these brown women age so well.) Mrs DaSilva was confined to her bed for most of the time and no one saw her except the three people aforementioned and her little niece Lily. Lily, who was so crying and upset from the moment she stepped from the buggy crying, everybody who witnessed it said though she was whisked into the house so fast, and everyone thought it was bad for the child about to be born to have someone as miserable as Mrs DaSilva's niece about all day long.

Everyone knows that the baby in the mother's stomach is susceptible to the external environment (so says the very latest medical advice as those of us who read know) and must have no disturbance before it is born; that the mother is to be loved and petted and indulged and made to feel happy and grand like a queen all the time. Have brought to her any little delicacy she should crave, even though her husband has to travel forty miles to get it, as Mr DaSilva had to travel to bring back hard-boiled booby eggs, which was all Mrs DaSilva craved having gotten used to them in Kingston, perhaps, where one does pick up queer habits. Isn't it funny how these women's cravings always seem to match their husbands' pocketbooks? For Lurline who works for me is in the family way right now, and all she has been craving is green mangoes sprinkled with sugar which is a very convenient craving for green mangoes are everywhere stoning dog, (as they say), and free for the taking which is a good thing for her husband Alfred is poor as a church mouse. I only hope she has the baby before the mango season is over.

I don't care what anybody says I have it on the best medical authority that it is bad for you to have your young cousin (or anybody) around you all the time crying, drowning (it might be said) your baby in her tears, and is it any wonder the baby came out the image of that Lily? And yet she seemed perfectly happy from birth (and loved and spoilt even more by her parents when they discovered that Mrs DaSilva could have no other, poor dear!). But it seems that the whole effect of her cousin Lily crying when she was in her mother's womb is coming out now, for when I looked carefully at her recently. I noticed, in truth, that she was looking careworn. For a young little baby girl her eyes have lost their freshness. They have dark circles now and her smile doesn't come as quickly as it used to. She practically has to drag it out and her mind is wandering, you can see she has to make the effort to bring her attention back to what you are saying. All in all, Lily has become one sad little girl, no matter how hard she tries to pretend otherwise. She is so nervous and jumpy: when her father himself put his hand on her arm the other day when he came to fetch her she jumped with fright. Literally! I saw it with my own eyes. What a strange reaction to have to one's own father! And whose hands did she think they were? It was the oddest thing. Why are her parents forcing the poor child to get into a boarding school where only white girls go? Is that what is bothering her? Lovely as Lily is they can't turn her into something she is not, you know. They will end up regretting it. Mark my words. Can't they see what they are doing to Lily?

II

. . . and always now the nightmare of his hands ugly and thickly covered with matted hair like some wild beast his hands holding the reins his hands at table carving the roast his hands holding the prayer book in church his hands unbuttoning . . . trembling . . . touching . . .

When the thoughts come crowding in she returns to the mama-lily game which she played endlessly as a small child in Mama's room with the high bureau with the pictures she had to climb on a chair to look at. The pictures in the double gilt frame of Mama and Auntie Lily. Mama and Auntie Lily so alike it was hard to tell them apart, so alike when she played the game of looking from one to the other ever so fast her head spun and they merged into the one she saw in the mirror every morning of Lily-the-child, as if she were their child. She felt guilty whenever she thought this, as if she were betraying Mama whom she loved more than anyone in the world. So why as she got older did she fancy that she looked more like Auntie Lily, wanted more and more to be with Auntie Lily, become Auntie Lily?

Was it because Auntie Lily was what *he* called (scornfully it is true) an 'Independent Woman', sitting there in her house in Burnt Ground which Aunt Mercy had left her. The wooden house by the river with the sign in blue and white saying POST OFFICE the windows on the verandah which had the big metal signs STAMPS and TELEGRAMS the notice board with official notices pasted up and which people came to consult every day (though most of them had to ask Auntie Lily what the notices said). Inside the post office itself the dark pigeon-holes with letters of the alphabet stencilled on for people's mail the telegraph machine which Auntie Lily knew how to operate Auntie Lily sitting there at the centre of the universe connecting through bags of mail which came and went by telegrams which flew through the air by the red mail van which carried the King's Royal Mail to railway stations connecting her with the trains that took you everywhere. And though they had not seen Auntie Lily in years, since Mama had quarrelled with her last time they visited, she could not shake out of her life the image of Auntie Lily beautiful in a thin, nervy wound-up kind of way with her quick movements entering things in books, counting the government's money at the end of the day and locking everything away carefully Auntie Lily being careful about everything even her smiles her hugs her kind words her laughter as if she had to ration them (for whatever reason) and became afraid and withdrew into herself (you could feel it) if she felt she had exceeded that day's ration.

And since she no longer cared what *he* said or thought she would like to become an 'Independent Woman' too with no mother no father around just herself alone with upswept hair and ledgers and books and her piano for she would never never give up her music as Auntie Lily had.

III

Lily, they said, had the sweetest voice in the land, a pure soprano that could hit all the high notes and break crystal and startle birds. Lily sang not only in her own church, but was invited to concerts and socials and rallies at the churches around to sing sometimes with Mr Abbott, a baritone. Their voices blended perfectly with Aunt Mercy as chaperone. And because Lily was young and slender and beautiful all the young men would stand outside the post office even when it wasn't open, hoping to get a glimpse of her or hear her voice or the cascading notes of the piano. Sometimes in the wooden house by the river, Lily sang only for herself, totally unconscious of the commotion her singing caused. For instance: all the duppies in the graveyard who were getting ready to haunt people one night stopped dead in their tracks at Lily's singing. (It was the only thing that had any effect on them outside of garlic and asafoetida.) And Mr Shepherd in the shop across the road from the post office once weighed out a pound of sugar over instead of under-weight and gave the wrong change – in the customer's favour – when Lily's song came crossing the road (and people regarded Mr Shepherd's behaviour as a greater miracle than that of the duppies!). When Lily sang at night trees crowded nearer to the house to hear her (being careful to move back by morning), and the soursops and mangoes ripened faster and one night, (you might find this hard to believe), one night an Ol'Higue was getting ready to shed her skin so she could fly off to suck a baby's blood, and at that moment Lily's song came passing by and Ol'Higue's skin started to shiver so much at the sound it refused to leave her, clung to her tightly so Ol'Higue couldn't get out of her skin and fly that night. O the magical things that happened when Lily sang!

Aunt Mercy knew that the young men hung around the post office just to see Lily, so she never put Lily out front to serve the customers if she could help it. She made Lily sit where only the tips of her shoes and part of her skirt could be seen from the window. (And the young men still found that provocative!) Lily sorted the mail, wrote things down in ledgers and dealt with the telegraph system which always confused Aunt Mercy. Lily didn't mind, she was so very happy, her hands were light as high notes. When she hit the telegraph keys her life hummed all the way down the line to her message's destination and back up again. When she stamped letters her touch was so delicate you hardly heard a sound. If she did handle the customers she greeted them most charmingly and read their letters to them quietly in a corner where no one else could hear, whispered them even, and made no comment nor lectured them about the contents and embarrassed them as Aunt Mercy sometimes did. And Lily laughed at the young men who were in love with her (but not to their faces of course for she was also kind), especially Mr Abbott the baritone with whom she sang, and who was a man of substance (forty acres, a horse and buggy) and from a respectable family (otherwise Aunt Mercy would never have allowed them to sing together) and who wished to marry her. But Mr Abbott though nice, was short and *plodding* Lily found. She didn't want to hurt him so she was gently turning his interest in the direction of Turah who was not beautiful and not terribly bright, but whose family had a lot of land and who was described as rich and who loved Mr Abbott dearly.

Lily paid no attention to the village boys she had grown up with because Lily was young (just seventeen) and felt she had her whole life ahead of her. Lily hadn't been exposed much (beyond the church socials and musical evenings) but Lily was well read. She had consumed all of Aunt Mercy's library (*In Durance Vile, A Maiden All Forlorn, Lady Verne's Flight* by Mrs Hungerford) and all of Miss Delevante's (Ouida's *Ariadne, Moths* and *Friendship* were favourites) and all of Teacher's Wife's (*she* preferred Mrs Alexander's romances). This was unfortunate since Lily was romantic even without the literature and shared many confidences with her girlfriends, Amy and Jasmine, on the back verandah facing the river when the post office was closed (whispered because Aunt Mercy listened in on everything), and they agreed that there could be only one possible destiny for Lily which was that one day this tall, dark, handsome stranger would come riding by, come ask for Lily, come take her away (where, they were not yet sure) to live happily ever after. Lily knew this would happen with such certainty that this secret knowledge sustained her happiness day in day out. She hummed as she worked and the telegraph lines hummed too as they took her messages to the world that she was waiting and waiting and she hummed as she stamped the letters lightly as kisses, imagining that every one was to or from her waiting lover, her Prince Charming . . .

So Lily was not surprised when he rode into the post office compound one day, on a bay horse as she had imagined, and he was tall and handsome with a lovely waxed moustache and elegant clothes and deep penetrating eyes that raked Lily so hard she felt instant pain. So hard that she almost forgot to greet Mr Dalrymple the post office supervisor for the parish, an old friend of Aunt Mercy's and almost like a father to her, and he introduced this gentleman Mr Pym from P&T headquarters, doing a tour of the island to write a report on facilities.

But Lily didn't believe for one minute that he was really from P&T though she admired the strategy he had used to come and meet her. And from the moment his hand touched hers Lily truly honestly could remember nothing of the rest of the day, the night, the next morning when he rode off in a mist after promising to love, honour, cherish her for the rest of their lives. To return, shortly, to break the news to Aunt Mercy, to take her away . . . completely forgetting what happened there behind the big rock at the river that night, completely forgetting about sneaking out of Aunt Mercy's house (the first time she had done so) to wait for Mr Pym (Harold to her), putting it out of her mind completely in her misery at not hearing from him although a few months later it all came back terrifyingly real when Aunt Mercy, worried about her, how thin and nervous she had become, how dark the circles under her eyes, had taken her to Dr Dampier in Mandeville and he confirmed that Lily was pregnant.

Pregnant? How could that be? For Lily hadn't the faintest idea of cause and effect since no one had told her the facts of life.

Aunt Mercy's reaction was totally lost on Lily for all that mattered was that he had gone without a word, had not replied to the letters she sent him from the post office endlessly, thickly bunched as clouds; she'd heard nothing, nothing. At first she could not believe it, fantasized about accidents, amnesia, his being recalled to England to be knighted by the King and finally after Lily had had no word no word and was going mad, she did something unthinkable, criminal even. She sabotaged in a crude and childish way the telegraph system so that Mr Dalrymple would have to come and put it right and she could thus get news of Mr Pym, (selfishly cutting the village off from the rest of the universe and worse, destroying HM Government Property – a £5 fine!).

When Mr Dalrymple came he did not see Lily, who was indisposed and lying in the darkness of her room, but she leaned her forehead against the painted wooden wall that divided her room from the parlour and heard Aunt Mercy ask (quite casually) what had happened to that nice Mr Pym. Mr Dalrymple said that Mr Pym had had a big promotion in the colonial service and had been sent to the Andaman Islands to reorganise their postal system there. Aunt Mercy was mystified as she had never heard of the Andaman Islands and Lily never heard where Mr Dalrymple said they were located (if he ever said). For she had flown to her school Atlas and couldn't even find it in the gazetteer (though in truth it was a small Atlas and not everything could be included, surely) but how could someone be promoted out of one's life to a place people had never even heard of? And she thought for the first time as she sat listlessly leafing through the Atlas of Mr Pym who had such freedom to stay or to go just like that to the ends of the earth while she, she would always remain here hemmed in by mountains linked only by the hum of the telegraph wires, deflowered, trampled, defiled, besmirched, soiled (for the vocabulary of her reading remained).

For the first time in her life Lily looked at herself, at her body, her brown hands, and though her skin was lighter than Mr Abbott's or her friends Amy and Jasmine's, than most people's in the village, and though her hair was so long and thick it could be piled up respectably on her head with virtually no padding, for the first time in her life she realised that there were other, superior, attributes which resided in whiter skin, straighter hair. In belonging, not to a poverty-stricken little colony, but to Mother England where the King resided. That in the world in which she lived these attributes, these alone, conferred power and freedom.

And she no longer felt beautiful, sharp and crisp with clean edges ready to slice through life but dirty, smudged, second rate. Unlike Mr Pym she couldn't do as she pleased, fly out of reach of responsibility, fly from trouble, fly to a new life elsewhere. She was mired in a little village in a little island that Andaman Islanders had never heard of, as stuck in the mud and dirt as Eglantine who had twelve children for eight different men, as Myrtella who had had seventeen (thirteen dead) or Gem and her brood with not a one to mind them, all the women she, all the respectable girls, had once so despised, now she was as fallen as they were. And at that moment she couldn't figure out precisely whether she was suffering like this because she was a woman or because her skin was not white like Mr Pym's.

Now she hated to go into the post office for she couldn't stand the hum of the telegraph wires the clatter of the keys and when (after it was all over) she came back for what else was there to do her fingers were like lead on the keys the wires never sang any more when she stamped letters her hand was as heavy as Aunt Mercy's 'THUMP THUMP-THUMP THUMP' she never smiled at the customers and was sometimes rude when they asked her to read their letters told them to come back even when she was doing nothing and was becoming every day more and more like Aunt Mercy. The worst thing was that Lily stopped singing. Lily never sang again though the young men kept hovering around hoping to hear her. But Lily's song never came and after a while they drifted off to other homes where the girls were more congenial. In the evenings now the space outside the post office stayed blank and enigmatic and Lily liked it so, for it affirmed that the Lily she had been, the young innocent girl, the beautiful singer, no longer existed.

The older people were not as mystified by the sudden change

in Lily. Because Lily was such a good girl and Aunt Mercy such a hawk watching over her no one, not even the worst gossip, suspected the real reason for Lily's illness for they didn't have to look that far. They had seen cases like Lily's before – singing happily one day, wasted by mysterious illness the next. When Aunt Mercy sent Lily away to stay with her sister Mrs DaSilva who was expecting and needed company and left her there for several months, the more knowing understood that Aunt Mercy had done it to get Lily away from the evil forces sapping her life. For shortly after Lily left, that Turah married that Mr Abbott whom everybody knew was so sweet on Lily they would have made such a fine couple and everybody knew that that Turah's people dabbled in spirits. How else could they have acquired all the land they had in such a short space of time? It was clear that that Turah and her family had obeahed Lily so that Turah could get Mr Abbott who was the best catch for miles around. And everybody secretly gave Aunt Mercy advice on who was the best obeahman to consult to get the spirit taken off Lily (and *thrown back* on that Turah and her family they strongly advised). And Aunt Mercy who gossiped about everybody's business but never revealed her own, accepted their sympathies and smiled thinly saying *yes yes true true* to everything. And made her own plans for Lily.

My Dearest Aunt Dawn,

I hope this letter finds you in the very best of health. Sister Lucy and Mr DaSilva likewise. I have not heard from Lucy for ages but I know she is busy with her Harvest Festival coming up and everything. Well my dear Aunt, I write to you with a *heavy heart* on a matter I never thought in my *wildest dreams* I would ever have to deal with. But Auntie, not to beat around the bush, Lily is in the *family way*!! Can you believe it? After all the care and attention I gave her from the very day her mother died and left her an orphan. (You know only too well the story of her father if he can be called that.) Believe me, Aunt Dawn, I wanted to kill her. The hardest part is *there is no one here I can breathe a word to*! Now I understand what you and Mama and Aunt Vera went through when Lucy had her 'accident' (?), but of course Lucy has always been lucky and has risen above all that. *Some of us have our bread well buttered*!!! Poor Lily is a shadow of her former self fretting and fretting. I am trying not to be too hard on her though *she's broken my heart* and every day I have to deal with the public with a smile, as if nothing has happened, and you know more than anyone else *what other heartbreak* I have had in my life. I blame myself, though God knows I kept the most careful watch over Lily except for the *wolf* that actually *came in sheep's clothing*. Totally deceived me. But no matter. Lily is still a good girl who's had her head turned by an unscrupulous calculating man (*as happens to the best of us*).

Auntie, the only good thing is that the father is not one of the common people around or I would never be able to hold up my head. He's a very handsome Englishman with a *big job* in the colonial P&T. Not a little nobody so I guess we should be glad for small mercies. But my dear, he packed his bags and left the country shortly after it happened. So there's *nothing to be expected* from *that quarter*. In any event you know the history of these white men and our women. They might plough and scatter but they do not practise husbandry (*as Papa used to say*).

My first thought was to marry Lily off to *somebody*. There's a nice young man here who's sweet on her, one of Dan Abbott's boys. Beautiful voice and quite respectable if you remember the family, though a little dark and *hair not the best*. But Lily will have none of it. I hope she doesn't end up *hating all men*, for that happens, *I know*, and though you see her there as such a meek, obedient little thing underneath she has her grandmother Elie's will and once she has made up her mind *there is no moving her*.

But my dear Aunt, can you imagine my disappointment? No one to turn to but you. Can you talk to Lucy and see what you can do? I'm afraid to write to Lucy directly for the letter might fall into Mr DaSilva's hands and I know how jealous he is. Do you think Lucy would take Lily to stay with her until the baby is born? Aunt Dawn *I have to get her out of here.* Apart from the fact that Lily's made this one mistake (*paying dearly too!*) not one of us is above reproach and I don't want to ruin her chances for life. Lucy came out of her trouble well didn't she? Do you think you could work on Lucy to take the baby since she can't have one (*God forgive her!*). She's not too old. In this modern age women are having babies up to a ripe old age and Lucy's not yet thirty.

Anyway Aunt Dawn I believe I have given you the picture. I leave *everything* in your *capable* and *blessed* hands. Please write immediately. *I am going mad* with anxiety. Just say the word and I will send Lily.

Your affectionate niece
Mercedes

PS I have written this letter *with such a heavy heart* I have not enquired properly about your dear self. I know you are still getting up at all hours to deliver babies every which way. *What a blessed woman you are.* More than a mother to Lucy and me, to everyone. Please be more that a mother now to our darling sad and very unfortunate little Lily. MN

PPS Make sure to tell Lucy that the *father* (scoundrel that he is), is a very handsome *Englishman* so Lily with her good looks is bound to have the most beautiful baby in the world and *white* too. I hope it is a *boy* for girl children have such a hard lot in life. Look at Lily, Lucy, all of us. As soon as a boy is old enough he can get on his horse and ride away and nobody says anything but the girls are the ones left behind to carry the burdens. MN

IV

. . . there goes Gabriel Martinez flying past galloping his horse like he's crazy again he's sure to break his neck one day everybody says and Gaby is so crazy he might do just that but I wish that I were allowed to ride my horse all the time and gallop like that on the road and not just trot sedately in the pastures only one day you know I would take off flying and never come back, fly into the winds, the clouds, fly to Auntie Lily . . .

IV

. . . Gone! Just like that! Not a word to anyone till Mr DaSilva became really alarmed when I sent the news to him at the saw-mill at tea-time and he and Jackson started a proper search and he heard that people had actually seen her galloping her horse down the road. When I heard that my blood froze my stomach started acting up again. I feared the worst, expected to see them bring her broken body back home (for an accident was all I could imagine and no thought for *my* feelings). But he and Jackson came back empty-handed. They found her horse tied to the hitching post at the railway station. She knows she's not allowed to ride on the road alone or gallop. Cool as you please she left a note with the stationmaster to say she had taken the train to go and see her Aunt Lily. Just like that! I know that woman is behind it. God forgive me if I'm wrong, but the child has not been the same since we came back from that visit two years ago. I swore we would never go there again. I would wipe her memory from our lives. It was clear as crystal she was doing everything in her power to seduce the child away from me. For weeks afterwards little Lily could talk of nothing else but her Auntie-Lily-this-Auntie-Lily-that every blessed day until I had to slap her real hard one time she vexed me so.

That Mercy must be laughing in her grave now. To give me so much happiness – only to have it snatched away again. Something she prayed for to get back at me for Robert Merriman, I never took him away I swear to God. He was the one that came after me. From we were children Mercy was jealous of me. With Marjorie it didn't matter. Marjorie was the quiet one but Mercy was hard as nails and terrible. She had to have everything, she never forgave our parents for having me and taking all the attention away. I couldn't help it that Papa and Mama, everybody loved me best for everyone said I was the prettiest and brightest of the Neal girls. It's not my fault that she was jilted at the altar by that Robert Merriman. He probably found out at the last minute what a terrible scheming b---- she was, though I never told him anything about her as God is my judge. But she never forgave me after all these years and I never even wanted him. She bided her time. She knew how badly I wanted a child, how badly she was playing on that when she sent our niece Lily to me. To receive that new-born child into my arms was as if God was giving me a chance to be reborn myself. To show he had pardoned me for the sin I'd committed. I admit it now I was very wrong but I was young, so young and innocent, and Mama and Aunt Dawn and Aunt Vera in Kingston (especially Aunt Vera) between them completely took charge of my life, told me what to do. I was so sick with fear to have my life ruined. My God, I'd have done anything and afterwards, the disaster, the pit of despair, knowing that I had ruined forever any chance of ever again conceiving.

When Lily came nobody knew how broken my life was, not even Aunt Dawn, for I was too ashamed to tell her. After I found out I just continued to hold my head up high. Walked about as if I owned the town. My husband Mr DaSilva busy making a family with that woman over at Salt Spring. It didn't stop with the marriage. She made a baby nine months after our wedding the most lavish this town had seen.

When Emmeline Greenfield, that dried up old maid, told me about it I thought she was being an awful b---- getting back at me after all these years because the Christmas Bazaar I organized the year after my marriage, when she broke her leg, had been so successful far more successful than any of hers everybody said. And after that it was just expected that I would organize the Christmas Bazaar and everything else because I do have a talent for organizing. Her nose was put out of joint no doubt about it. She just refused to take part in anything after that, going on and on about how glad she was that I had come to relieve her because now she could concentrate on her intellectual pursuits (such rubbish!). Even though I suspected her motives when she told me this story, there are times in your life when you know that the worst thing you can possibly hear is the truth, and I went myself to the woman's house. Rode over there and didn't even bother to dismount for playing in the yard were Mr DaSilva's children. The spitting image. I wanted to kill myself. On the way back I took a shortcut by Rider's Pond and thought of throwing myself in, but when I considered what the Lord had already pulled me through I knew he had put me on this earth for a purpose so I swallowed my pride.

But it was separate bedrooms from that day on. I didn't have to say anything to Mr DaSilva. He knew. Someone had seen me outside the woman's house. He doubled the housekeeping allowance that month. I was free to charge anything I wanted. I could extend and redecorate the house to my heart's content. I admit I had more peace of mind for I didn't have to worry any more about meeting the demands of the marriage bed now that I knew he had someone else to satisfy his lust. I didn't have to worry about where he was when he strayed. I thanked that woman for rescuing me from something I submitted to only as my wifely duty. But O God, I couldn't stop my longing, my craving for a child. I kept hoping that by some miracle the doctor who had told me I could never again conceive was wrong. Of course when Mr DaSilva and I first started to share the marriage bed he fully expected me to bear children. For some things are best left untold, Aunt Dawn had warned me.

Sometimes the thought that there were so many children in the world and not a single one was mine was really unbearable. So when Aunt Dawn came to me with this story of Lily being with child I didn't hesitate. It was as if the Lord was answering my prayers. How could I have known that I was being used by that Mercy, by that Lily herself who could not have been as childish and innocent as she seemed for here she was crying like Rainstorm, docilely agreeing to everything, then having the baby and refusing even to look at her. Packed her bags and left

without a word. How's that for a mother? It was only out of pity
for her that I called the baby Lily. Mr DaSilva suggested it. He
said she was white and perfect like a lily. Just to see the
expression on his face, the tenderness with which he greeted her
when he held her in his arms made up for all the past sorrow
of my life, for all the nervousness and anxiety of the last six
months. For it was tricky business that though Mr DaSilva
helped me through it all. That's one thing I must say. He fully
understood that we had to shield our little cousin Lily from
scandal.

And God has been good to me all the years since. Good. He
gave me the loveliest most beautiful little daughter in the world
such a lovely child. She gave my husband a renewed interest
in our home. He became such a wonderful father. I forgave him
all his past transgressions even though he continued to support
his family at Salt Spring (I knew that but it was only right and
proper). Since we have had Lily I don't think he has ever been
with that woman again. I believe he loved little Lily even more
than I did. God knows our lives have been blessed, blessed over
these years until that last visit with that Lily at Burnt Ground.
Such a sneaking wretch. What I blame myself for now is that
I did not have to stay in touch with her at all, did not have to
take Lily to see her (for she had said she would never again visit
us).

The first time I took little Lily was when Mercy was dying
and wanted to see her. Lily was five years old. We were so close
I had even forgotten she was not my natural daughter. I felt no
fear at all in taking her to Burnt Ground though Mr DaSilva
was not too happy. He didn't want me to go, he would have
preferred it if I had no contact with my family at all. But I said
no, blood is thicker than water. We had nothing to fear from
Lily for she had willingly without a murmur given up the child,
showed no maternal instincts at all and the child of course
would never know. And when we got there, that hard hearted
wretch paid the child no more attention than she paid the little
black children passing by, she has such a cold spirit. I came
back feeling pleased that I had overcome this hurdle so well for

I had always feared this first meeting between Lily and her natural mother, feared (silly me!) that somehow there would be some magical bond. That they would fly towards each other like magnets.

But nothing happened and after that Lily and I kept in touch for now we were the only two left in the family. I kept her informed of little Lily's progress, encouraged my daughter to write her own letters as soon as she could. Little did I know what a dark pit my goodness of heart was making me dig for myself. We only visited twice after that. The next time I went for Mercy's tombing. It was the least I could do. And then two years ago when Lily was nine, on impulse, I decided to visit Burnt Ground for a week.

And that was the biggest mistake I ever made for suddenly the two of them were as thick as thieves giggling over the slightest thing as if they were both children. Sometimes when I saw their heads together bent in the same lamplight my stomach contracted for there *was* this magical bond, this magnetic force drawing them together. My stomach was ruined from that time! I spoke sharply to my niece about what she was doing but she played the innocent. She always does. I was forced to cut short my stay and take little Lily home to preserve my sanity. God knows what evil that woman planted in the child's mind for the nightmare started only a few weeks after she came back home. She was perfectly alright for a while, then I noticed she was not as warm and loving and open as she used to be. Her eyes lost their sparkle, her teachers, everyone, noticed it. She suddenly went from being this bright, happy little girl beloved by everyone, the most beautiful and popular in our town to a ghost of her former self. She got nervous and jumpy and started to have nightmares and, O God, she began to imagine things, to tell such lies, she even said her own father. . . . I cannot even think of it, this man who has been more than a father to her, who has given her everything who has been so loving so good . . . she began to shrink away from him as if he were a leper at the table. She hardly raised her eyes from her plate anymore, it was unbelievable, as if some evil spirit had taken control of her. I prayed to God every night to tell me what was really wrong with my little Lily. How best to deal with it. She went from loving her Papi so well: she would rush out of the house the minute she heard his horse in the evening crying 'Papi! Papi', she would cling to him for the entire time until he tucked her into bed and told her stories. I never in my life saw a more loving father. And I felt better when I realised that Lily had started to become a woman early; all the girls in our family did. The doctor said that that was accounting for her skittishness, said nothing but growing pains, just be patient with her.

Her father and I we tried hard to be kind and loving to put up with her sulks and silences for we knew it would pass. But the way she shrunk from her Papi was more than I could bear. And then she got the idea firmly into her head that she wanted to go away to boarding school. My little Lily at boarding school, when we had all agreed that she would be taken in the buggy every morning to Miss Foster's like all the other respectable girls around! Lily suddenly wanted to go to St Catherine's (and I know it's Emmeline Greenfield's influence for that's where she went, she is always telling you – 'the best girls' school in the island'). And I would like my baby to get into the best girls' school in the island. What a triumph it would be especially over that Elsie Montrose. Her girls would not stand a hope in hell of getting in. They are not taking in girls *that* dark no matter who they are. But I don't want my baby to go far away from me.

I know it's the influence of that Lily for all of a sudden our little daughter cannot bear to be with us in our home again, cannot stand her father, cannot stand her mother (for she hardly speaks to me, even) and she has been pestering me and pestering me again about visiting her Aunt Lily. I couldn't imagine it was so important or I'd have swallowed my pride and taken her. How can she hurt me so? Mr DaSilva wanted to get into the buggy and go for her straight off. I never saw a man more angry in my life and fearful, yes. And what is there to fear? (O God I won't think of it.) I calmed him down, reminded him that we must avoid a scandal at all cost. Both he and Cousin Lily are so strong-willed, one never knows what would happen if they met. We must send Jackson with a suitcase tomorrow. We will say it was all planned. In a few days when she has got visiting her Aunt Lily out of her system I will go and fetch my baby back home.

VI

My dear Aunt Lucy,

I expect you have received my telegram saying that Lily arrived safely, though I have had no reply, and the hurried note sent by Jackson when he brought her clothes, for which Lily is grateful. She herself has not written for reasons that will become clear below though, believe me, I have encouraged her to do so. I am sure (from your silence) you believe that I instigated this, but nothing could be further from the truth. She gave me the surprise of my life by arriving on the mail van (though I must confess that I feel enormous pride at what a grown-up young miss she is and so resourceful!). But when I learnt that she had come without your permission I was very angry indeed and planned to put her on the train the very next day. But as I explained in my note and Jackson could tell you, Lily woke with a fever next morning (you needn't be alarmed she is perfectly fine now) and then over the course of nursing her and listening to her and may I add becoming increasingly alarmed over her mental state, certain things came to light that have so shocked, revolted and alarmed me that I will find it impossible to send Lily back until I have expressed myself to you and your husband, in the most open way possible, and have received certain assurances from you both concerning Lily's welfare.

Yes. Your husband, Aunt Lucy. I am aware you have no secrets from him (and I presume, he from you, you are such a perfectly matched couple). So I am sure he will read this letter; indeed, it is imperative that he should do so. And when you have both read, digested and talked over what I have to say, I am sure you will recognise that it is in your interest to destroy it — if only for little Lily's sake — for I believe her future happiness and well-being must be the foremost consideration. Indeed, if this were not so, I would not bother to communicate with you at all. I would keep my child with me as I should have done from the start, do everything in my power to turn her against you both. (At this stage it would be easy considering what you both have put her through.) But after my initial shock at what has been revealed to me, my horror, my rage, and, yes, after all these years, my tears, I forced myself to think rationally, something that is conveniently omitted from the upbringing of us women (otherwise my God how we would challenge the world!) and I have come to the conclusion that I could make no possible claims on Lily without telling her the truth. And I do not want to be the one to introduce another trauma into her life while she still has to get over the effects of the first.

Yes, *trauma*, my dear Mr DaSilva for I see you sneering. You never could stand the thought of a woman being more than a willing body, could you? Trauma, my dear Mr DaSilva, being a word not likely to be in your vocabulary but now firmly fixed in mine from my reading of Doctor Sigmund Freud the great Viennese psychiatrist, whose brilliant works are stirring the world (I am sure you have at least heard of this controversial figure since you are such an avid reader of the Sunday papers). It is only from the new understanding which I am gaining of human nature (including my own), that I am able to see you not as the inhuman beast you undoubtedly are but as a very sick man, and on that basis I can feel for you, yes, even sympathy. Trauma is what you have inflicted on poor dear innocent little Lily by your sick, vicious behaviour which has turned you from being (in her eyes) the person she most trusted and loved to one she now confusedly fears. You can be assured that I have got every word of the beastly story out of her even though she herself does not fully understand it all, thank God, and I have tried my best not to alarm her. But may I assure you Mr DaSilva that should Lily return to your house and should you behave towards her in any way beyond that of the most scrupulous and caring father, I personally intend to abandon Doctor Freud and take a pistol and shoot you until you are very dead and then, Madame-Faithful-Wife, I shall tell the story to the world. I mean it, Aunt Lucy.

Oh, don't worry, I knew from the very first what kind of man your dear husband is (though I never in my wildest dreams knew how really depraved). Even as I came to your house in my state, already carrying my child, that man could not contain his lust, wanted to seduce me then and there. I can now talk about it openly for I have had many years of loneliness since then when I have done nothing but exorcise those demons. But can you imagine my horror at that time, my feeling – after my recent experience of male betrayal – that all men were brutes? I probably would have turned into the typical man-hating female like Aunt Mercy after *her* experience (which you Aunt Lucy are very familiar with), if I had not in my loneliness and despair managed to turn my mind to higher things, thrown out the foolish romances, the foolish longings that had so inflamed my youth and, under the influence of the new headmaster here, Mr Patrick and his wife, started to subscribe to a higher kind of literature from Coopers Educational Bookshop and Circulating Home Library in Kingston. (I would certainly commend its services to you Aunt Lucy for you are sorely in need of something outside of your little world of tea parties and good deeds.) But then you don't even know what I am talking about. You, Aunt Lucy, sold your soul a long time ago for some canisters of silver and some solid mahogany furniture and a closet full of expensive clothes, for things called 'status', 'power', 'respectability' conferred by a marriage of Mr DaSilva's money and your own overriding ambition. Yes, I know about you, Aunt Lucy. In her dying days all Aunt Mercy ever talked about was you (how you must have scored her heart!). But do not worry, she must have found peace at last for her dying words were, 'God forgive Lucy . . .'.

But God will find it hard to forgive Lucy for her newer, greater sin, ignoring the grief and pain of a little girl, blinding her eyes to the truth for to admit the truth would be to let the scales fall from her eyes, to admit her life was a sham and her husband a monster who could not control his lust (or have it sated) even on his honeymoon – who still travelled to see another woman even as he promised to love, honour and cherish her. Oh, don't think his second family is such a secret, Aunt Lucy, even we in Burnt Ground know about it for people are interested in the doings of the great and the near-great far more than they are of the humble.

Yes. There was a time in my life when I was made to feel that what you have (the husband, the house, the position) were all a young woman of my background should aim for, and were it not for my 'fall', I suppose they would have materialised, for 'tree don't grow in my face', and I didn't lack for admirers. My only regret is that I was brought up so that I did not see the other possibilities, didn't know that a woman didn't have to fulfill any of the roles laid down for her – servile wife, old maid postmistress or slut. I was so under the thumb of Aunt Mercy that I didn't even know I could think for myself, (as indeed, Aunt Mercy, you and my mother were in your time totally oppressed by your mother and your aunts). And this is probably why despite everything I have such a tremendous sense of optimism about little Lily (at her age I would never in my wildest dreams have shown such independence of spirit as she is showing, would never have dreamed of going away to school as she dreams – so limited was my world). And when I talk to this little girl I am amazed at her knowledge and the breadth of her under-standing, the receptivity of her mind, astonished to see material-ising in my own daughter some of the very ideals for which progressive women are now fighting (gall and wormwood to you, I know, my dear Mr DaSilva).

And while I'm on the subject, since little Lily is so anxious to go to St Catherine's, I would like it to be accepted firmly by you both that this would be the very best thing for her. Quite apart from anything else she needs to get out of that house and gain other exposures (and of course she also needs to get away for other reasons). She tells me that you are both dead set against it (and I can see why) but if she is accepted, please let her go. Little Lily is already lost to you – and to me – by the very process of change that is sweeping the world, changes both good and bad, and of which, despite our best efforts to shield her, she is already the inheritor.

I too am caught up in these changes for you might be surprised (and relieved) to know that I plan to leave very soon for Colón. Sneer again, Mr DaSilva, for only the most common people are going to such places, you will say. But on that score you are wrong, for not only labourers but people of quality are now leaving this country, the flower of our island – businessmen, professionals, doctors, nurses, teachers, ministers of religion, are going or have gone. And why not, for what is there to keep us here?

Unless you are already well established in this country, unless you have birth, colour, position it is virtually impossible for a young person just starting out in life to realise any ambitions, to rise above the poverty – and the minds – of their parents. This country for centuries has been drained of its lifeblood to build up Mother England and the white people there. Nothing has been left for the coloured races, nor are we given a chance to prove ourselves, to have a stake in our land, to feel that anything, anywhere, is our own. The people who rule and reap in this country are the Governor and the clique surrounding him at Kings House. And that is why we must seize the opportunities opening up elsewhere: in that great democracy called America or in our neighbouring Latin Republics where the spirit of free enterprise is tearing down the rigid caste system which we still have to put up with at home. Do we not see, day after day, wherever we live in this country, the visible results of what travel to foreign parts can do to liberate our people's minds? I myself have seen the young men, even the young women I went to school with, girls who started out with far less than I did, returning from 'foreign' in two or three short years with so much more than I could ever have. Not in wealth, (for that is not my concern) but in their air of sophistication, of knowledge, of new ways of seeing, of doing, and they make me feel so backward and provincial that I am sorely embarrassed (I who once thought I was the epitome of knowledge and sophistication!).

And one thing the notion of travel has done is stirred in me longings that have been dormant for so long I never knew they still existed, the feeling of being trapped, hemmed in, that I used to feel as a young girl (and which was probably responsible for my 'fall' in the first place), the feeling that outside of this village, this island, a world awaited me if only I could fly. I felt at age seventeen that my life had ended for I had done the unpardonable (though why it was not only pardonable but expected in women of the so-called lower classes was never clear to me). And I still regret that I had not the courage to do what my heart, my mind, my very being cried out to do, which was to keep my child, come what may. Do you, Aunt Lucy who have accused me of being hard-hearted, do you think it was easy? To leave her behind, take the train and come back to my room in Aunt Mercy's house, my station at the post office as if nothing had happened?

Increasingly now I realise that my life did not end at seventeen and is far from over. Granted that I am no longer in the first flush of youth but I am still a woman of feeling, of desire (sneer again, Mr DaSilva) with aspirations which still can be fulfilled – even to bearing other children – but which will only be fulfilled if I have the courage to create my own wings and fly.

I am sure I am embarrassing you my dear Aunt Lucy and you Mr DaSilva, but then I have always done so for am I not the living reminder of things you would rather forget? I do not apologise for baring my soul (though I did not intend to) nor for speaking so frankly (you might say, cruelly) to you. For I want you to understand me and understand me so well that you will have a better appreciation of what I want for little Lily.

Lily with all her knowlege is still the total little innocent and I think if properly handled can rise above what has happened to her (caught, fortunately, in time) without too much permanent damage, if you are both willing to ensure that this is so. And that means, dear Aunt Lucy, that you need to put your responsibilities as a mother over and above your responsibilities as a wife and social arbiter (come what may). You need to take a good look at your husband and see him for what he is, and take steps to protect your daughter from further harm. Although I intend to be out of the country for a while, do not think for one moment that I will not be present in spirit to watch over Lily. At the first hint that things are not right with her, I will take whatever steps are necessary to protect her (even if it means paying the supreme penalty).

And since I have expressed myself so fully (far more fully and frankly than I intended) perhaps the time has now come for you both to express yourselves, to assure me of your good intentions, your desire to make amends for the harm you have both done Lily and that there is no possibility of a recurrence. You can only do this by finding yourselves here next Thursday morning 19th inst. so that I can meet you face to face. I know this demand will be onerous to you both, especially to Mr DaSilva who is not used to taking orders – and certainly not from women – but who has placed himself in a position of having no choice since my vow of never setting foot in your house remains stronger than ever, except in the most extreme circumstances affecting Lily.

You both know me to be a woman of my word and so have my assurance that if you choose to come in a peaceful and calm manner and discuss Lily's future with me, I will lay no claim on Lily (over and above that of the sympathetic aunt she considers me to be). In other words, I will give Lily back to you. But if you choose to ignore me, I promise, I will take my daughter and I will tell the truth, first to Lily and then to the world (and what a feast the Emmeline Greenfields would have!).

At the same time I think we should recognise that Lily might not wish to go home with you just yet, and I think my library and crayfishing in the river are equally competing attractions so I would like it to be a condition of your coming that Lily's wishes in this matter be honoured. If she chooses to stay a while longer, I assure you, I will endeavour to predispose her to going home as best I can, and return her well in time for school (in any event, the date of my own sailing is fixed).

I am sure, dear Aunt Lucy, that you will choose to reply to *this* letter, if only by your presence here next Thursday.

Believe me, I remain
Your sincere Niece,
Lily

VII

Now the visitors have gone, an air of excitement, of expectancy, hovers about the house by the river. Leaves hold themselves in readiness as for rain and the birds are shushing one another. Trees start to move in closer, though surreptitiously, and even the duppies in the graveyard stop jostling for positions and grumbling among themselves. The river stops rushing and the world holds its breath until all is quiet.

From inside the house comes first the sound of a piano (badly out of tune) then the clear, unmistakable sound of Lily's voice not heard for over a dozen years. We had forgotten its beauty so cannot compare it now to what it was. We just close our eyes and let ourselves soar with Lily's song.

But what is this? Are there two Lilies now? For softly, softly, faintly at first, comes another voice, piercingly sweet as a child's, joining our Lily's, getting stronger and more assured as it sings a descant to our Lily's song. Two voices, perfectly matched, perfectly blended. Can there be a sweeter sound in the world than Lily, Lily singing?

O if only that Emmeline Greenfield with her superior knowledge acquired from books, with her formidable social inheritance, with her elegant turn of phrases (in foreign languages too), if only she were here to give to the world a truly inspired version of this magical moment. What a story she would tell!

Summer Lightning
and other stories

Olive Senior

Olive Senior is one of Jamaica's most exciting creative talents. *Summer Lightning* is her first collection of short stories.

Her setting is rural Jamaica; her heroes are the naïve and the vulnerable, who bring to life with power and realism issues such as snobbery, ambition, jealousy, faith and love.

Written in vivid, colourful detail, these rich, compelling stories recreate with sensitivity and wit a whole range of emotions, from childhood hope to brooding melancholy. Each is told with an affectionate and poignant perception of you and I at our best and worst. Gently we are led, laughing, crying, but always enjoying.

Longman Caribbean Writers Series
ISBN 0 582 78627 4